Grace
and the Secrets
of the Beech
18

Judi Stephenson

Grace and the Secrets of the Beech 18

Published in 2013 by Lavender Sky Publishing LLC

Copyright (c) 2013 by Judi Stephenson

ISBN-13: 978-0-9893519-1-1
ISBN-10: 0989351912

Printed in the United States of America

Acknowledgements

This book is dedicated to my spectacular mother, in celebration of all that she is and the extraordinary women who raised her. And to my dear father, who supported and provided for his family, no matter how difficult.

Thank you Jeff and Scott for encouraging me to try harder and reach higher to stand where you stood. And to Judy Ballard, Jeff, and Callie for creating such a beautiful cover design.

I would like to acknowledge Kit Campbell for editing as well as Torrey and Emmett for their wise contributions.

Thank you John, for your patience, support and love.

As for Laura, Suzanne, Casey, Jill, Liz, Suzi, and my aviation pals, I greatly appreciate your backing and friendship.

In remembrance of those incredible Women Airforce Service Pilots from WWII!

Contents

Chapter 1: Into the Sky   1
Chapter 2: Grounded   5
Chapter 3: Hangar One   13
Chapter 4: Henry   19
Chapter 5: Beached Betty   25
Chapter 6: The Familiar Path   33
Chapter 7: A Visit With Betty   45
Chapter 8: Buckle Up!   47
Chapter 9: Only A Dream?   61
Chapter 10: Freedom   71
Chapter 11: Up For Adventure   75
Chapter 12: Forbidden   81
Chapter 13: A Minor Setback   85
Chapter 14: October Skies   95
Chapter 15: Perseverance   99
Chapter 16: The New Kid   105
Chapter 17: Troublemaker!   129
Chapter 18: Henry's Place   139
Chapter 19: A New Friend   153
Chapter 20: What About Dorothy?   169
Chapter 21: Final Flight.   197
About the Author   213

Chapter 1: Into the Sky

I leaned forward to peer over the metal nose of the airplane between the blur of the propeller blades. I could see where the white centerline met the horizon, but I was straining to see the painted pavement just three feet ahead.

My father's voice resonated through the headset hanging loosely around my ears. I tried to ignore the sounds of the engine and the propeller swirling air around the cockpit in order to focus upon Dad's instructions, but it was impossible. I nodded intently anyway, which seemed good enough for him.

Flushed with adrenaline, I watched Dad's hand point toward the dashed white line and then motion to the far end of the freshly paved runway. Everything outside the airplane was moving in slow motion. Even the morning sun heating the pavement stirred slow patterns in the air, waving them lazily over the deep green grass lining either side of the path ahead.

The world was in stark contrast to my pounding heart. I took a deep breath and attempted to calm my anxious nerves. Then I raised my eyes to meet the polished, deep blue sky. It welcomed me.

My right palm was moist with perspiration as I gripped the throttle in my palm and tightened the muscles in my right leg to lessen its trembling. Though the belt across my lap was taut, the silver knob fastening it to my shoulder strap kept coming undone and scorching the bare skin on my arm. Dad reached over and calmly reconnected the metal hinge and then smiled, giving me a thumbs-up signal.

Even though I was taller than most of the students in my class, it was a struggle to see over the instrument panel and reach the rudder pedals at the same time. I had argued adamantly against using the vinyl cushion sticking to the back of my t-shirt, but it did shorten the distance between my heels and the rudder pedals. And since the pedals actually steer the airplane, I acknowledged the awkward cushion as a necessary evil.

Dad had a duplicate set of controls on his side of the plane, so I found some comfort in the fact that if he reacted quickly enough, he could save us from skidding off the side of the pavement and nosing over a perfectly good airplane. But I had been practicing this, right? It was time for me to manipulate the controls without anyone helping me.

I was suddenly aware of Dad's hand cupping my own, forcing me to slide the orange-handled throttle forward. The plane turned a bit to the left and I quickly remembered to step on the right pedal. My actions were too forceful and the nose jerked back to the right and I had to ease the pressure. I had to get a feel for it.

My father shifted his own pedals slightly until we were pointed straight again. We gathered speed and the trees began to blur out of focus. Then Dad's hand pulled away, entrusting me to hold the throttle as far forward as it could be. All of a sudden, the pedals were moving against my own weight. It was all up to me.

The world moved by faster and faster and any sudden footwork would send us careening toward the edge of the pavement. For the first time since we turned onto the runway, I actually heeded my father's instructions.

"Ease it off gently," Dad said.

I pulled lightly against the yoke and the ground began to fall away. The end of the runway was soon beneath us and all I could see was blue ahead. I was flying!

We climbed and climbed into the sky. I noticed lakes and rivers I had never seen before when my feet were bound to the Earth. It was like I was flying for the first time. Though Dad had let me fly with him before, that day was different. The foothills looked like green, carpeted anthills and I was sure we were level with the stony peaks to the west.

Dad taught me how to turn, how to climb toward the sun and then glide toward the cornfields below. He showed me how to trace invisible circles over the ground with the airplane and then point the nose back to the sky.

After spending the better part of the afternoon in the air, Dad said it was time to turn back to the airfield. He told me to pull the throttle out and begin a descent. As I pulled the handle, the nose dropped toward the Earth and I panicked for a moment, pulling back on the controls. Dad motioned for me to let go of the yoke. I released my grip and the nose lifted slightly, and then lowered to begin a shallow descent on its own.

"Grace," Dad said, smiling at me with understanding, "the airplane is like the birds soaring above the airfield. It already knows how to fly.

Chapter 2: Grounded

It's funny how a place can hold onto a memory, I think to myself as Dad and I bounce along in the front seat of his red pickup truck. The day Dad let me perform the takeoff in his Cessna without his assistance was the true beginning of my love of flight. I always think of it when we drive this route together. And it is the only thought that can possibly bring a smile to my face right now.

We are heading down the familiar stretch of road, which leads to the town's oldest airfield for what feels like the millionth time this summer. Dad has an airplane repair shop on the field and, though it's a Sunday, he has some projects to finish and I have to tag along.

At fourteen, I'm too old for a babysitter, but Mom refuses to leave me home alone all day if she has to work. So, if I'm not quick to make plans with one of my few friends she approves of, I have to go to Dad's house, which means I have to go to the airport because that's where Dad spends most of his waking hours.

My mood lightens as we reach the corner with a faded stop sign. It's the only intersection on the drive to the airport that sits right beneath the departure path of one of the runways. Some days, people will be parked in the ditch off the side of the road, watching bellies of airplanes pass overhead. My parents did the same thing with my brothers and me years ago.

Dad rolls the steering wheel through a wide left turn and I look to see if any airplanes are taking off.

Any other morning, it would be routine to go to Dad's shop with him. But today happens to be the very last day of summer vacation; the same day my friends and I take our annual trip to the water park in Denver. It's the most memorable event of the summer, a final celebration of freedom from fluorescent lights, early sunsets, and homework. Unfortunately, I got in trouble with my mom last night, so I'm stuck spending the day at the airfield. Again.

I'm still pretty upset about the whole thing. Not because I'll be starting high school tomorrow, which is intimidating in itself, but because I have whittled away my favorite months of the year out here, pacified by the thought of the water park trip. While Dad fixes airplanes, I figure out how to pass the time out here by myself.

One good thing is Dad doesn't really fuss over me. Sometimes he even gives me a couple dollars to clean his workshop. Also, his girlfriend isn't keen on spending her day around oil and grease, so she doesn't visit Dad at work very often. Cindy pushed her way into his life less than a year after my parents divorced. Mom is convinced she frequented the diner Dad stops in for coffee every morning until he finally asked her out.

All I know is, had I been smarter last night, I would be screaming down a water slide right now.

The paved road leading to the airport eventually turns to rough gravel and Dad's rusty old red pickup exaggerates every bump it hits and then continues to vibrate for a few more minutes. The long seat cushion taking up the length of cab is like a springboard. Part of the floor is rusted out, so I can see the road whizzing by below us.

Dad is over six feet tall and whenever we hit a good-sized pothole, it sends him to the roof of the truck. Today he has pushed the seat far back, allowing his long legs to stretch out as he rests his right hand on the steering wheel. In his left hand, a cigarette hangs precariously between his fingers. I watch as he pauses, narrowing his eyes as he inhales the white smoke.

For years, I've been after Dad to quit the nasty habit, but I don't have the energy to argue with him today. Besides, he finally agreed to cut back. Now he just lights up while driving. In the summer when the windows are down, the smoke isn't so bad, but in the winter, it makes for a cold and smelly commute. I figure at least he's giving it some effort.

"Good morning to fly," Dad says, tearing his eyes from the airplane crossing above us to focus on the road.

"I guess so." I shrug back.

Dad exhales stale cigarette smoke and I can feel his eyes studying me. "What the heck did you and your friends do last night, G? How'd you manage to get grounded for an entire month?"

"I don't know, Dad. I didn't think it was a big deal." I stare out my open window, hoping to drop the subject.

The late morning heat is already creating tufts of clouds over fields ripe for harvest. Soon the soft, cottony white forms will grow like mushrooms and then darken to an ominous gray. I've witnessed it countless times. The sky crackles and roars, and then douses the plains with a Colorado afternoon thunderstorm. The wind can nearly lift a person off the ground some days. And there have been times when the lightning has struck one of the cottonwoods surrounding the airport, sending a flash of light across the entire field. It makes the hair on your arm stand straight up.

No matter how quickly the storm forms or how fierce it becomes, it leaves a whisper of beauty across the mountains and prairie in its wake. Rainbows light up the fields as the smell of cool damp earth lifts up into the atmosphere. Greens glow vibrantly and butterflies come out of hiding to drink from moistened wildflowers. Everything is renewed and fresh.

Dad snuffs his cigarette out in the ashtray beneath the AM radio. The tin holder is spilling over with cigarette butts and one more causes ash to clutter the air between us.

"I haven't seen your mom that angry for a while, G." Dad sighs. "But I can't say I've been around her all that much lately."

"I had a slumber party and we all got hungry," I reply, withholding as much information as possible, in case he takes Mom's side.

"What'd you do, rob a pizza delivery boy?" Dad laughs.

I look past him, ignoring his joke. The mountains are a purplish blue and layer behind one another, building up to two rigid peaks that have watched over these plains for countless years. I wish we were going in that direction.

"Well, what happened?" he asks again.

"Nothing really. We were just hanging out in a tent in the backyard and we were starving, so we rode our bikes to the gas station and bought some food."

"Hm, a bunch of young, teenage girls riding their bikes around town at night? That doesn't sound like a good idea."

"It wasn't that late, Dad."

"Alright, well, give me the rest of the story then."

"There is no story." I look straight ahead, maintaining my innocence. "We just stayed out for a while to watch the meteor shower. I should have spent the weekend with you and this wouldn't have happened."

"Meteor shower, huh? I didn't realize there was one last night." Dad comments as he glances up at the sky.

It isn't like I committed a crime. I didn't steal anything or sneak alcohol or even toilet paper any of the homes in the neighborhood. Some friends and I just set up a tent in the backyard and told ghost stories until we ran out of popcorn.

Mom doesn't buy anything resembling junk food, so the five of us decided to ride our bikes to the gas station to stock up on all sorts of goodies. On our way back home, we got distracted. My friend Karla mentioned a meteor shower that was supposed to start around midnight, so we climbed the hill at the end of the block to get the best view. It's the part of the neighborhood where civilization meets wilderness, and it was the perfect place to watch the debris light up the night sky. It was a warm night and we must have stayed for a while, because we all fell asleep out there.

As we tried to sneak back to the tent with flashlights and what remained of our liter of soda, bag of potato chips and five-cent candies, Mom was waiting for us. Standing outside talking to the next-door neighbor with car keys in hand and sculpting apron still tied about her waist, she scolded me in front of my friends. Apparently, Mom had spent the last hour driving through town searching for us and she was two minutes away from calling my friends' parents, which would have been bad.

She made us pack up the tent and come inside to sleep on the living room floor. But the real punishment came this morning, after my friends had gone home.

I wasted the better part of this warm September day arguing my case against the most stubborn woman in the world. If only I could make Mom laugh when she was angry, like my brother Dennis could. One minute she would be furious with him, and the next minute, Dennis would have her laughing so hard that she would forget what he'd done in the first place. I, on the other hand, am powerless to sway her anger. So instead of taking me to my friend Lynn's house this morning for our water park adventure, Mom dropped me off at Dad's. She stepped inside long enough to tell him that I would be spending the day under his supervision, restricted from television. And that he was to have me back in time for dinner, when her shift at the store was finished.

It felt like I was standing inside an icebox as I watched Dad sit quietly in his recliner chair, newspaper in hand, unable to cover his surprise at seeing his ex-wife. Since their divorce, it was rare for Mom to spend more than thirty seconds around Dad. But things got worse when Cindy came along. All communication ceased between them. And just when I thought they might begin a conversation this morning, Mom turned and opened the swinging screen door, letting herself out without another word.

"Well, I don't think your mom's going to let you stay with me for a while, Grace," Dad says, fetching another cigarette from the pack in his shirt pocket.

"What? Did she say that? But you're the only one who gives me any kind of freedom, Dad!"

He ponders my last sentence. "Yeah, well, I probably give you too much freedom. She's just protective of you, G. Your brothers are out of the house now and you're still her little girl...our little girl."

It's surprising to hear Dad defend my mother.

He looks over at me and his forehead crinkles. "I'm really impressed that you haven't been bored out of your mind at the airport all summer long."

Truth be told, I am bored out of my mind some days. Summers were different at the field a few years ago, when my older brothers were around to stir up adventure. The three of us would build forts in broken down airplanes or take turns stealing cookies from the old welcome desk. We dared each other to stand as close as possible to the runway and watch the larger planes blaze into the sky. Once, all three of us were running in the grass as fast we could, hands pressed over our ears, trying to keep pace with a huge plane roaring down the runway. It took about thirty seconds for Dad to discover our antics and ban us from getting anywhere near the paved strip after that. So we forged our playground in the hills and fields beyond the airport, where we had to use our imaginations.

My oldest brother, Tom, graduated high school a few years ago. He's attending college in a town about an hour south of here. And he has a steady girlfriend, so I rarely see him.

Dennis, our middle brother, finished high school in May and has been working for the Forest Service over the past summer. He shares a cabin with a few other people in the mountains and works from sunrise to well after sunset, saving money for his first year of college.

So it has been, for an entire summer. I have wandered the airfield and the surrounding prairie and foothills mostly alone. Sometimes I'm allowed to bring a friend. But then they're stuck at the field all day too, and that gets boring, especially if they aren't fond of airplanes.

The pickup truck rambles over jagged railroad tracks as a fox darts across the road in front of us. All but its tail disappears in the tall weeds. Whenever I cross these tracks, I fix my eyes for as long as I can in one direction, following the rails into the horizon, and then switch to the other side.

To the east, the train tracks disappear into a hayfield, only to be swallowed by the earth. But to the west, the two shiny rails wind around and climb the Rocky Mountains into a fresh world of adventure. If ever a train happened to stop and I was given the choice of which direction to travel, I would surely follow the sun.

I imagine the westbound tracks winding through the steep rock canyons and treacherous mountain passes, where valleys filled with aspen trees and untouched waterfalls filter their way down onto the stones below. I would watch herds of deer quietly grazing as they turned their heads to see the stream of rail cars pass across the afternoon. Finally, when the journey came to a close at the edge of the Pacific Ocean, I would continue by sailboat to discover the world.

Chapter 3: Hangar One

The muffled roar of an airplane distracts my thoughts and turns my father's eyes to the sky. Whenever Dad hears a propeller slice through the air, he traces the winged frame behind it. Chances are good that he knows the pilot, or at least the airplane.

Dad dodges a pothole as he passes the main hangar on the field and parks in front of the big white cinderblock building that he rents for his repair shop.

"Some joker parked in my spot," Dad mumbles to himself as the dust cloud around us begins to settle. A blue sedan is gleaming in the section of dirt beside Dad's hangar.

"Whose car is that, Dad?"

He flips up the sun visor and then gathers the clipboard at his side. "I don't know. I haven't seen it out here before."

The rounded roof of Dad's building bears a yellow sign that reads, "Hangar One," in large letters.

The name is ironic because Dad's hangar was actually the second building to set its foundation on the airfield over fifty years ago. It has been home to many a winged machine. It even housed gliders for the military during World War II.

The structure is smaller than the two other hangars on this side of the airfield, but it definitely has the most character. And it's the only one whose walls are made of cinderblock. The rest are made of metal and wood and tend to rust easily.

Dad replaced some of the wood on the rounded ceiling himself, though much of it is the original Douglas fir. The strong, amber planks rest on the cement walls and follow the curvature of the roof, supported by a sturdy frame of thick wooden beams that are wide as tree trunks. Even the bolts holding the beams together look like the ones that hold old railroad ties to the rails, as their iron heads are the size of a quarter and have rusted into a dark amber color. On the outside, the roof is protected from the elements by a ribbed metal, making it look similar to the other two hangars out here.

Dad is the sole mechanic on the airfield and he has rented this shop for at least ten years. When I was younger, he served as apprentice mechanic to a man named Don under this very same roof. I was pretty small, but I remember the black and white sneakers Don always wore and how kind he was to my brothers and me. He kept the refrigerator stocked with sodas and a jar filled with candy bars in his office for the three of us. Don became good friends with my father and even attended some of Tom's basketball games.

Then one morning, Don announced that he was going to retire to Florida with his wife and buy a sailboat. He offered Dad a fair price to take over the business; Dad signed the lease and has managed to stay busy ever since.

I snatch up my sweatshirt and glide off the seat of the cab, slamming the door of the truck closed as Dad fetches a twelve pack of soda from the back. I had expected to see the main hangar door open when we drove passed it. Men are usually standing inside, polishing their shiny airplanes and waiting for someone to converse with. After all, it's nearly noon on a Sunday, the most social day at the airfield.

"Pretty quiet out here today," Dad says, motioning for me to grab the grocery bag on my side of the truck.

I nod. "I was thinking the same thing." On an average Sunday, there is at least one engine humming overhead. But on the ground, there are almost a dozen airplane owners who regularly swap stories around Dad's hangar. I don't see anyone waiting for him today. Not Jeff, the former aerobatics pilot who owns a shiny red biplane. Not even Neil, the ruggedly handsome crop duster pilot who usually has Sunday afternoons off, but still comes out to the field to visit with Dad. Karl, Randall, Greg, and Vaughn: none of their vehicles are parked in the lot.

A car door shuts and I turn to see a man strolling toward us from the direction of the blue sedan. He is much shorter than Dad and balding, with a wispy strand of grey hair fluttering around his forehead. He is dressed in dark blue pants and a long-sleeved shirt with a yellow and blue striped tie. For some reason, I can picture him sporting a polka-dotted bow tie instead.

"Paul Markham?" the man asks in a loud voice.

Dad frowns and tucks the soda under his arm. "That's right. What can I do for you?"

The man walks up to Dad and puts his right hand out. "Ted Skylar, Stonebrink Development. Nice to meet you, Mr. Markham."

A look of disgust flashes across Dad's face as he shakes the man's hand and nods. "Hello, Ted. What brings you out here on a Sunday?"

"Oh, I was just in town and took a detour to check out the area." The man looks up at the sky and then toward Dad's hangar. "I guess Sunday's a quiet day out here, eh?"

"Not usually this quiet," Dad replies, emotionless. Then, looking down at Ted's obnoxious tie, he says, "I didn't know you guys worked on Sundays."

Ted tilts his chin up and stands with his weight on one leg while the other is bent casually. "Oh, well, I suppose we aren't too different from you. Just trying to make a buck."

"Humph." Dad smirks.

"Anyway, Paul," the man says, changing the subject and shifting his weight to both legs, making him seem less arrogant, "I saw you drive up and thought I should introduce myself. Oh, and I was going to put this under your door, but I'd rather give it to you in person. That way I could put a face with the name, you know?" The man hands Dad a large envelope and then nods at me. "Is this your daughter?"

Dad struggles to maintain a friendly disposition. "Yes, it is. She's spending time with her old dad today."

The man smiles at me. "Nice to meet you. I hear your father's a legend around this airport."

I shrug my shoulders and look at the man's wisp of hair fluttering about. "Yeah, I guess."

After an awkward pause, the man says, "All right, well, I'd

better get going. I'm on the south side of Denver and I sure don't need to get in trouble with the wife for missing supper." Ted turns on his heel and walks back to his car, pausing to wave as he opens the car door. "Nice to meet you. You folks have a pleasant day."

Dad nods and watches the car back out of the lot, following it until it disappears down the dirt road, stirring up dust in its wake. He looks quizzically down at the envelope in his hand.

"Was he from the company that wants to buy this place, Dad?"

"Uh-huh." Dad sighs and starts walking toward his hangar, muttering to himself again. He places the soda on the step below the door to the hangar. "Grace, help me get the rest of the things out of the back, would you?"

I set the grocery bag down next to the soda and follow Dad back to the truck.

Dad isn't just the sole mechanic out at the airfield, he's also the resident psychologist, marriage counselor, and unofficially elected leader of the pilot group. So I suppose it makes sense that the guys appointed him to lead the fight against the development company intending to buy the airport and turn it into a middle-income neighborhood. As if he doesn't spend enough time at the airfield already, now he's out here every day making phone calls and putting a plan together to save the field before he even begins his workday.

Dad's change of mood is immediate. It's obvious that Mr. Ted Skylar with the yellow tie represents the bad guys.

It would be devastating to see this airfield get torn apart, with its rich history dating back to the 1920s. When it was opened, businesses in town supported it financially. They hoped that the new field would bring tourists and airshows, drawing crowds of people, and thus more customers to the growing town. Dad found some old posters advertising the airshows when he was helping Don move his things, and now they're hanging throughout his office. Many of them are from the 1930s, and judging from the images, they are from a time when the public viewed aviation as sensational and intriguing.

"Do you think those guys would really demolish the airport, Dad? I mean it seems like the town would want to make it a historical place or something."

Dad smiles faintly back at me. "I don't think many people know this field is even out here anymore, G. There hasn't been an airshow since the college came in and took over operations."

"Well, maybe you could put one on, Dad. I'd advertise it at school and I bet all my friends would come. We could make enough money to buy the land." The idea is actually exciting. The last airshow took place in 1970, two years before I was born, and I still hear stories about it. All sorts of old warplanes were out here and so many townspeople bought tickets that they had to extend the dates to accommodate everyone.

"We'd need a lot more than one airshow to make that kind of money, G." Dad's smile grows wider. "But if you want to, you could head over to the research hangar and see if they'd approve one. You have more enthusiasm than any of the guys out here."

I didn't think about having to get permission. Several years ago, the college built an enormous hangar on the northeast corner of the airport and they use it for atmospheric research, leaving the three "old hangars" on the other end of the field to Dad, Henry, and the rest of the renters. We're so far away that I sometimes forget the college actually owns the field and have to approve anything that happens out here. It has actually been a great situation for Dad and the college has maintained the field nicely, so it's too bad they've decided to move the research center to a larger airport.

The low rent that the college has charged Dad has been the only thing allowing Dad to stay in business at times. When the field was privatized, many renters relocated and Dad had to slash his repair rates to retain customers. Now many of them have become his close friends and faithfully return to him because they trust his work. A couple weeks ago, I overheard Dad telling his buddies that if the development company has its way, he'll not only be out of a shop, but he may have to move out of the state due to competition. That would be bad for all of us.

Chapter 4: Henry

I set the last package of supplies down on the cement and catch a glimpse of Henry. His white hair reflects like snow in the early afternoon sun as he fumbles to open the side door to his hangar.

"At least one person is out here," I observe out loud.

Dad looks over at the old man and pulls his keys from his pocket. "It looks like Henry is at it again, huh? Maybe I can catch him before he leaves."

"Dad," I ask, "does Henry *ever* leave?"

Dad laughs and unlocks on the door to his own hangar.

It has always been curious to me that Henry has been out here longer than any other renter, and occupies the largest of the three hangars on this end of the field, but no one I know has been inside it. Of course, Henry has a house in town somewhere, but the old man spends a great deal of time by himself in that big metal building. It must be freezing in the winter. Dad's hangar is half that size and it is impossible to keep the icy January wind from finding its way through every crevice.

Henry's place is similar to Hangar One with its white metal, rounded roof, but the old man's is rusted in spots and supposedly houses a low-winged airplane that he cannot fly anymore. I'm not sure what else is hidden beneath that sloping roof, but fear prevents me from investigating. My brothers have told me some pretty scary stories about the old man and though Dad assures me none of them are true, they left an unforgettable impression.

Dad says that Henry's medical certificate expired years ago, so the old man hasn't been able to fly legally for a very long time. To pass the hours, he rebuilds worn-out airplanes, but because of the arthritis in both of his hands, his progress is slow. On weekend afternoons, Henry sits in his faded lawn chair, watching airplanes taxi around the grass near the front of his hangar as they prepare to take to the sky. It's not a very busy field, but it must be better than staring at a television set from a dusty recliner.

Another of the many rumors circling the airfield is that Henry was a World War II fighter pilot. I don't know if that's true, but he owns three airplanes from that era that sit, parked in the dirt and weeds, near the west edge of the ramp. The planes rest beside his hangar and, sadly, they have been parked so long that bird nests are poking out of propeller hub while rabbits dart in and out behind the worn tires.

The first time I ever actually got close to Henry was the time my brothers dared me to climb into one of his old airplanes. My two cousins were out at the airfield with us that day, which made it even more difficult to turn down a dare. It wasn't until I was halfway to the plane that Tom yelled at me to watch out for snakes and I could hear my cousin, Kirsten, giggling. Being that I am much more afraid of spiders than snakes and that it was too late to back out, I moved stealthily toward the old plane. My audience watched, safely hidden behind a tree twenty yards away.

The weeds were tall around all three planes. I traipsed through the stickers, beginning to regret agreeing to the dare after all. When I had pictured snakes, they were those garden types with the long, yellow stripe down their scaly backs, the kind that my brothers would catch near our house. But hadn't someone seen a rattler out there just the week before?

When I reached the door of the single engine plane, I tried to move the handle. It gave a squeal and broke off in my hand. Woops. I pressed my finger into the gap and tried to release the door, but it was locked tight.

I couldn't give up that easily of course. I looked back at my brothers and they were laughing, but my cousin was pointing at something. I thought she was motioning for to me to try the other door. Embarrassed that I didn't think of that, I rounded the nose of the airplane and as I ducked away from the propeller blade, I nearly ran head first into Henry! My heart leapt into my throat and stifled my voice.

I stood, trying to think of an explanation as to why I was breaking into his airplane, but there was something odd about the old man. It was like he didn't even see me. He kept pacing back and forth beneath the wing, mumbling something to himself. His pale blue eyes were vacant, looking off into the distance. I wanted to run, but I couldn't. My legs were heavy and my mind was moving slowly, like gears that wouldn't engage. I was contemplating my next move when the old man registered my presence.

"Who are you looking for?" Henry shouted in a stern voice, his long gray eyebrows furrowed.

I stood still, shaken by the tone of his voice and unable to think of a reply.

"They've all gone back to the barracks," he shouted again, waving his hand toward the tree.

From my position beside his plane, I watched Henry walk slowly back to his hangar, mumbling and gesturing to the air the entire way. The confrontation dissolved any interest I had had in climbing inside the tattered old airplane. There was something melancholic about Henry that day and I felt guilty for violating his privacy.

When I fought through the dense weeds to get back to the tree, my brothers had vanished and I could just make out the back of my youngest cousin trailing behind them. Tom and Dennis knew, just as well as I did, that the last place we wanted to get caught is anywhere near Henry's hangar. Dad says he has a special punishment for that. Thankfully, none of us ever figured out what it was. We were all too afraid of the old man.

The second time I ran into Henry was the only other time I have seen him venture more than fifty yards from his hangar. I was alone, sitting at the picnic bench inside my father's shop; half-heartedly working on a history assignment that was making the inside of my eyelids pretty appealing. Truly, I was aching to be finished with it so I could go outside and visit the tree swing near the canal and get some fresh air.

I wasn't sure how long Henry had been standing inside

Dad's hangar, but I jumped when I saw him. He didn't seem to notice. He just stood in one spot, admiring a silver tail-wheel airplane that needed lots of engine work and had been keeping Dad really busy. I do remember that Dad had some colorful words for the old beater, being that it was nearly fifty years old and had seen much better days.

That day, I sat and watched Henry in silence. It was like spotting a deer in the tall weeds. I couldn't help staring at him, studying the man whose hangar is a few hundred yards away, but is rarely seen up close.

I thought I was being sly, but then Henry looked right at me and asked in a hoarse whisper, "You going to learn to fly this thing, kid?"

I smiled and shook my head, amazed at how different Henry was the second time around. Even from the distance that separated us, his blue eyes were vibrant and his entire face was smiling at me, so different from the day I almost knocked him over in the field.

"No sir, my dad is teaching me in his Cessna," I replied, pointing at the airplane parked outside.

Henry dismissed Dad's newer plane with a wave of his hand and looked back at the silver airplane parked on jacks in front of him. He revered it like it was an old friend that he longed to sit down with again.

Closing his thoughts, he looked up at me and winked. "Naw, you're tall. You can learn to fly in this old bird." Raising his thick, gray eyebrows, he said, "She'll give you a run for your money, though."

I was so taken back by his engaging manner that I couldn't think of anything to say. I just smiled back at the old man.

"Well," Henry ran his hand along the tail of the plane, "I actually had a question for your father, but I'll come back some other time." He pretended to tip his cap and smiled again so that I could see his straight, white teeth. "You keep studying, kid," he said, pointing at my book. Then he tapped the silver rudder and went back the way he came.

I sat, staring at the space where he had stood, replaying our brief exchange in my mind. That was the last time I saw Henry for a while. It was the only time I have ever seen him inside Dad's hangar.

Chapter 5: Beached Betty

Today I watch Henry open the side door to his building across the field and disappear inside as Dad loads the packages into his refrigerator.

For someone who has survived the various changes out here, Henry sure isn't social with the rest of the renters. Most of the time, Dad has barely turned the key in the door when one of his buddies wanders over with some kind of radio device or instrument in hand. "Hey Paul, what do you think about..." And as much as I enjoy flying, listening to the local pilots dish out their tales of near disaster gets a little dull on the third retelling.

I pick up one of the grocery bags and follow Dad into his hangar. As I step inside, I'm arrested by the smell of oil-soaked rags. Dad tosses them into a bin near the door and, when I stay with him, he brings the bin home and I wash and fold the rags as one of my chores.

"Oh Dad, those rags need to be cleaned," I say, making my way to the refrigerator.

"Probably so," Dad grumbles, reading through the contents of the envelope Ted had handed him a few moments ago.

"Is something wrong?" I ask.

Dad sighs and pulls at his mustache. "Oh, just that damned development company wants to have a meeting with all the renters. They have no idea how tough it is to get these guys together on short notice." Dad grimaces and walks into his office, tossing the letter onto the desk. "Or, maybe they do. Maybe that's the point," he says, taking a seat and looking at all the notes pinned neatly to his corkboard.

Though his hangar is the smallest on the field, it's amazing how much stuff Dad can fit in here. The office alone is roomy enough to accommodate a desk and couch. And outside his office, a refrigerator sits against the rear wall with a couple of picnic tables slid together in front of it. The tables are usually the center of activity.

In the far corner, Dad has expanded the bathroom and added a small shower for days when he wants to wash all the grime off before heading home. Really, a person could live inside this old hangar. And other than the two airplanes parked with sections of cowling and tires on the floor beneath them, Dad keeps the place immaculate. He is so organized that when he's finished for the day, he returns the tools to their proper places, recoils the cables and hangs them on the wall, files papers away and replaces the manuals on bookshelves. He'll even sweep the cement floor when he isn't too tired.

Dad tries hard to impose upon me his habit of keeping things clean and orderly, namely my bedroom, but it always seems like tedious work. Saturday mornings especially, the sun is calling me outdoors.

I look around the hangar, thankful that there's nothing to clean except the rags. I'm not in the mood today. "Is Cindy out of town again?" I ask, wondering if I can expect to see her face poking in any minute, since it is a Sunday.

"She spent the weekend with some of her friends in Estes," Dad grumbles from his office.

I'm glad. I really don't like making small talk with Dad's new girlfriend. I just don't have any interest in hearing how I should be styling my hair or what color to paint my nails. But the silence in here stirs my restless spirit. Maybe I should go and check on Betty.

Betty is the savior of the summer doldrums. She is the old red and silver twin-engine airplane parked at the very edge of the main ramp, facing west. An enormous cottonwood tree stands over her, shading her wings. It's hard to tell which one took the spot first, Betty or the tree. They seem to be old friends.

The cottonwood tree was supposed to be chopped down at one point to create more ramp space, but enough people protested to allow it to stand. As for Betty, Dad says that one morning she was parked there when he came in to work. I've heard a few men say that a skydiving company at another airport went out of business years ago and is still tied to the registration. It's strange that no one has come to claim her, though. Dad thinks that the owners didn't have the money to repair the timeworn airplane, so they left it behind.

The pilots around the field have affectionately named the plane "Beached Betty." That's because it is one of the many versions of a Beech 18 airplane, built in the early 1940s. The guys say that she'll never fly again. But, by the looks of things, Betty's spirit is not ready for retirement.

Despite the fact that her two main tires are nearly flattened onto the tar-creased pavement and her tail wheel has sunk into the dirt bordering the ramp, Betty spiritedly faces into the wind. The rope that binds her left wing to the ground is stretched and worn. It's as though the old airplane has turned to the right, hoping the northwesterly winds will lift her from her earthbound parking space. My father, the practical one, says that strong winds have caused the airplane to weathervane over time. I think he just doesn't recognize Betty's strength.

On closer examination, however, Betty has a few hiccups to take care of before she can wrestle the downdrafts again. The moveable surfaces on her metal frame are covered with a fabric that is weathered and torn into shreds for the birds to carry away. The metal that covers the rest of her surface is pitted with small dents and the trace of red paint that surely made her a beauty once has long been faded by the sun.

In spite of her cosmetic flaws, Betty stands taller than any man. The large frames encasing her two radial engines are silently awe-inspiring. The engines stand a couple of feet above my head and the metal circle enclosing them holds strong, seemingly impervious to time.

Throughout my many summer days at the airport, the old plane has been a faithful friend, serving as a place of recluse. I've transformed the back of it into my hideout, using cushions from an old couch Dad had in his shop. My favorite pastime, other than exploring the surrounding fields, is reading books on the steep upward slope of the airplane cabin. And I have spent countless hours sitting in the left seat of the cockpit, playing out flying adventures as storms build over the Rocky Mountain peaks and then pummel the airfield.

The rear of the airplane is covered with pictures clipped from magazines and taped over the ruined fabric. Sun-kissed beaches with towering palm trees, mountainsides dotted with wildflowers and waterfalls, every bit of which I yearn to explore. Old Hardy Boys and Nancy Drew mystery books decorate the floor. My brother Tom sketched images of sailboats and airplanes and posted them next to my photographs. From high up in the neighboring cottonwood tree, one can even spot a few of the sailboats from his drawings drifting across the lake nearby.

If the day isn't overbearingly hot, I'll open the door in the back of the plane and let the breeze carry through to one of the open panes in the cockpit. On those afternoons, Betty provides the perfect place for a nap, depending on the activity on the airfield. Her cabin is also the only space where I can be alone to write in my journal or escape all the tall tales that pass through Dad's hangar on a rainy day.

"Mind if I go visit Betty for a while, Dad?" I ask from the picnic bench as he makes some notes for himself in the office.

"Why don't you call your mom and see what time she gets off work, first. I forgot to ask," he says, standing up and weaving his way between the airplanes to the large, metal hangar door. "You're right G, the air is pretty stale in here." The door creaks loudly as Dad heaves it open and sunlight floods onto the cement floor. As if on cue, his friend Karl is standing outside, wearing a wide grin on his face.

"Well, good afternoon, troops. I was just about to knock." Karl greets Dad and me in his perpetually jovial fashion. He has the ability to make a joke out of pretty much anything, even if his jokes are pretty corny.

Karl shuffles inside the hangar, wearing oil-spattered coveralls. He is swinging a giant bag of hot dog buns in his right hand, while his left arm cups two packages of hot dogs tight to his chest. Anytime there is a picnic or airshow on the field, Karl is sure to be nearby. And if boisterous laughter is tracked to its source, one will inevitably find a cluster of people, sitting in on Karl's joke telling.

"Ooooh, Paul," Karl sighs as he loads his packages into the refrigerator in the back of the hangar. "I picked up a beauty of an airplane yesterday, and I need you to give her your blessing."

Dad sighs and runs his hand through his hair. It's a familiar habit he has. Whenever he's uncomfortable or wants to avoid a discussion, his hand goes through his dark hair, or he grooms his thick mustache. "I didn't hear you, did you just fly it in?"

"Nope," Karl replies, smiling. "I parked her outside yesterday after I picked her up. Didn't you even notice her shiny white wings on your way in?"

Dad shakes his head at Karl with exasperation. "Must have missed them." Karl has a peculiar gift for buying airplanes jinxed with some sort of problem for Dad to fix. Dad manages a grim smile. "So tell me, Karl, which plane did you decide on? And please don't tell me this is the 182."

Karl gestures toward a bright yellow and white airplane parked outside the hangar door. "Awe, come on, Paul, isn't she the prettiest thing you've ever seen?"

I cannot resist following the men outside into the sunshine. I'm curious to see Karl's latest find.

Dad looks unimpressed as his eyes move slowly over the single engine airplane. He stands for a minute, moving the left aileron up and down like he's deciding whether or not to get involved at all. "Did you already sign the paperwork?"

Karl puts his hands in his side pockets and nods. "Yup. He said there was another buyer interested, so I went and picked her up last night. I sold off my old 150."

Dad lets out a loud sigh, smiles at Karl, and then circles the brightly colored airplane. He pops open a door on the cowling to peek at the engine, then gets onto his hands and knees, taking a quick look at the belly.

Karl looks a little relieved as he watches Dad stand up and

open the door, peering inside the cockpit. "He'll change his tune when he sees the instruments she's got," Karl says to me, raising his eyebrows and nudging me with his elbow.

I smile back, but I know better. I've seen this exchange far too many times. Karl made a significant amount of money in the oil business and now has a hobby of finding airplanes in need of repair, to put it kindly. But he passes them onto Dad for the fixing part and the planes usually require a lot of time and attention. It makes for some pretty entertaining banter between the two men.

"Hmm." Dad crouches inside to look under the instrument panel and then pokes his head out of the cockpit. "I don't know, Karl. It'll take a couple days to get a good look." He unlatches a door in the other side of the cowling and squints through the small opening. "How's the maintenance log? Did you go though it before you signed anything?"

"Oh, it looks pretty good, I reckon." Karl's eyes shift to his shoes as he mutters, "I mean, it was really clean at first glance."

Dad looks up from the airplane and smiles at Karl, shaking his head. The two men carry out an entire conversation using their body language.

Karl runs his hand along the wing and sheepishly admits, "Ok, maybe the logbook looked a little too good. And I spose the signatures all looked the same on every page. You don't think he could have just filled out the whole book in one day?"

"Sure, if the guy didn't have a conscience and just wanted to get the darned thing off his hands." Dad grins at Karl the way he does when I tell him my homework is finished. "Have you noticed any quirks about it yet?"

Karl shrugs. "Well, I suppose there might be one...uh, sort of problem." He sighs loudly and looks over at Dad. "I'm having some trouble with the landing gear."

"The gear?" Dad blurts out.

"Well," Karl says, "the fluid looks good and the pump sounds all right, but every time I put the darned handle down, the wheels take their time coming out. The pump runs and runs, until finally I see a tire in the mirror." Karl frowns. "And it takes a long time for the gear light to turn green. I can't for the life of me figure it out." Karl is avoiding Dad's eyes now, staring at the dirt on his work boots instead. "You think you could just look over the gear this afternoon?"

"Ugh, you're kidding, right?" Dad drops his chin to his chest and shakes his head, and I notice a few grey streaks weaving through his dark hair. "I don't know, Karl." Dad points to the two airplanes parked near the door to the hangar. "I'm already running behind on these two and I'd like to have them finished today. And now I have to deal with that silly development company. Besides, the gear alone would take a while to go over. You know I have to get it up on jacks and swing it a few times unless it's something obvious."

Karl stands with his hands clenched around his overalls, silently imploring Dad. Then he offers, "How about I help you with those Stonebrink guys and you check it out tomorrow?"

Dad smiles. "Can you get the guys together for a meeting Tuesday night?"

Karl nods confidently. "Absolutely. Let me know the time and place and I will make it happen, Paul. Whatever you need, my friend."

"Alright," Dad sighs, eyeing Karl. "Leave it here in case I get some time after these two, but I'm not promising anything. Maybe I can get started on it tonight." He runs his hand along the edge of the propeller.

Karl looks at his feet again, waving back and forth like he's pondering his next statement. "Weeell, I was sort of planning on flying up to Sidney to meet a friend at Cabela's in a bit. I can try to make it back for hot dogs, but if I'm late, could I just leave her parked outside your hangar? Sound alright to you?" It's strange to hear Karl ask for Dad's permission.

Dad smirks, "do what you want, Karl, but I wouldn't be messing around with a gear problem. You might just end up setting it down in a field if those wheels don't come down, and what will you do then? It's not a good time for me to race out and pick you up. It's been pretty crazy around here." Dad says, giving him a stubborn look.

"It's a good thing there's no shortage of fields between here and Nebraska then," Karl says, laughing.

Dad shrugs and gives up on the argument. "The meeting's at seven o'clock in the east hangar," he says, walking back inside.

"Done." Karl lifts his chin, feigns a serious countenance, and then shuffles after Dad.

"I don't mind setting her down on a road, but it's those darn power lines that make me nervous, Paul," Karl says. "They seem to creep up when you least expect 'em. Remember when we landed that old Piper over the wires cutting across the road outside Greeley? I think we finally stopped about a hundred yards from the tractor trailer." Karl laughs loudly again and his belly shakes. "Boy, the poor guy must have thought he was seeing things when he climbed out of the cab."

Well, this is a story I've been hearing since I can remember. And it's my cue to go find something to do or it will be a painfully long day at the airfield. Anytime hot dogs are involved, beer is sure to follow and then conversations trailing until long after sunset. I walk out the door of the hangar and the fresh air lifts my spirits. Maybe I'll head out to the canal before I visit old Betty.

"Dad, I'm going to look for frogs," I say, walking out the wide, open door of his hangar.

"Don't kiss any, it's guaranteed to bring trouble!" Karl hollers after me.

I smile and remind Karl that I'm only fourteen years old, and then head outside to wander the fields surrounding the airport.

Chapter 6: The Familiar Path

A dirt path begins about twenty yards from Dad's hangar and looks pretty appealing at the moment. I need to walk off some of my frustration, so I follow the beaten trail as it winds through an open pasture and eventually leads to a canal with slow moving water and cattails growing high on either side. A warm breeze stirs through the underbrush, replacing any trace of crisp morning air.

I make my way to an area where the bank grows wider and the water drifts lazily beneath a couple of cottonwood trees. Wisps of cotton float downstream like gigantic snowflakes. The tall, green grass growing along the banks is fading into a bright gold beneath the late summer sun.

A few summers ago, Tom and Dennis hung a wooden swing from one of the branches of a gigantic cottonwood tree next to the canal. On the occasion I'm allowed to bring a friend out to the airfield, we spend hours leaping from the board into the waist deep water beneath. My friend Sunny and I fondly refer to the cottonwood as the "Friendly Tree." We once attempted to build a fort out of scrap wood from the airport and then attach it to one of the thicker branches, but all we managed to do was nail two boards to the tree before falling into the river, tools and all, laughing until our stomachs couldn't bear it.

The Friendly Tree stands as a cheerful contrast to a crooked, beaten-up ash that backs away from the water, pervading ominously over gnarled weeds and remnants of a small cornfield. Sunny and I have discovered strange things lurking beneath its twisted branches. Candles, mud-filled bullet shells and arrowheads are just a few of the treasures. We don't need much to ignite our imaginations as we attempt to frighten each other with stories about what has happened beneath the tree. The anecdotes are most frightening at sunset. I'm not allowed to be out here when it's dark anyway.

The swing sits vacant, waiting to be carried into another long, lonely winter, when its ropes will again bear the weight of ice and snow and its bench will warp beneath the moisture. I pull the prickly rope-swing toward me and leap onto the seat. The long, wooden board creaks beneath my weight and then settles down as I push back and forth, watching the riverbank for signs of life.

A black beetle scampers into the underbrush. Swarms of mosquitoes hover over the water. Two long, brown fish dart downstream followed by several smaller ones, staggered and fluttering in the current.

I take in the surroundings and kick my legs out hard, swinging high above the water until I'm startled by a low whooshing sound nearby. A great blue heron swoops through the air overhead. I must have scared the bird from its place of repose. I hear my mom's voice in my head, reprimanding me for disturbing the bird.

Mom would spend hours walking around all the tiny lakes near our old house, scouring the shorelines for herons. When she finally found one, she would wade through tall weeds and cattails, just to get a closer look at the creature. If she were lucky, the heron would pose long enough for her to sketch an outline of its form and then go home to sculpt it in clay. Mom even chipped one out of a translucent orange stone that glows like the sunset when it sits in the window. She sculpts a lot of birds, celebrating flight in its true, natural form.

As for man-made flying machines, Mom and Dad have very different opinions. I grew up hearing tales about my parents flying together, but I have never witnessed it. One afternoon when I was helping her pick strawberries from her garden, Mom told me about her last flight with my father in a small plane. It was about a year after Tom was born.

Mom and Dad had made plans to fly to Steamboat Springs to spend their first weekend alone together, leaving Tom with my grandparents for three days. The weather was beautiful on the day they departed. To get to Steamboat, they had to cross over the mountains, east to west, and Dad had mapped out the course over the lowest part of the terrain. The sky was crystal clear and the winds were light. Mom says it was a breathtaking flight.

Unfortunately, their return trip was a nightmare. The day began with Dad having trouble getting the engine started in Steamboat. After several phone calls and knocking on hangar doors, he tracked down the local airport mechanic's phone number. They had to wait a while for the man to get to the airport, as it was a Sunday.

The mechanic recharged the airplane's battery and helped Dad get the propeller turning. Dad thanked the man and took off for what should have been a fairly short flight home. Unfortunately, the delay was longer than he had anticipated. Morning had subsided to afternoon and it was nearly two o'clock before they climbed over the highest part of their route over the Rocky Mountains. Though Dad is certified to fly in the clouds, he tries hard to avoid it, especially over high terrain. Despite his efforts, my parents were soon engulfed by thick, white clouds and the ride was getting uncomfortable.

He knew he had little time before thunderstorms formed and dangerous downdrafts began, so Dad turned back toward the Steamboat airport, where they could safely await the storm's passing. Unfortunately, when he checked the weather report at Steamboat, low clouds and deteriorating visibility were being reported there too. Dad had no choice but to continue on through the white. And he would have to act quickly to plan his route.

Mom took over the controls for a while, buying Dad time to sort through his charts and coordinate with air traffic control. Until that day, Mom had relished piloting the plane above fields near their home. She was ecstatic when Dad relinquished the controls, allowing Mom to fly the entire distance to another airport for lunch and then helping her with the landing. Returning from Steamboat was a different story. Mom didn't have fun; she feared for their lives.

One moment, swift wind currents flooding off the mountains would lift the airplane hundreds of feet per minute.

The next moment, it felt as though they were breathlessly dropping toward the earth. She fought hard to keep the wings level until Dad was able to take the controls.

Retelling the story, Mom said she was so terrified that she promised herself when they did land safely, she would never climb into a small plane again. She said she couldn't bear the idea of Tom growing up without a mother. Disappointed and frustrated as he was at Mom's decision, Dad had too much respect for her to argue or press the issue. It wasn't until they divorced that he actually started teaching my brothers and I how to fly.

Dad wasn't blind to our fascination at all the airplanes visiting the field over the years. My brothers used to sit in whatever planes were parked in Dad's hangar and pretend they were airline pilots. And whenever Dad flew to another airport to pick up parts, I would refuse to go into the hangar with whoever was there to look after me. Instead, I plopped myself onto an old metal bench by the ramp and patiently stared at the horizon. I waited, straining to hear the sound of Dad's old Cessna powering back to the airfield. After what seemed like hours, his red and white airplane finally came into view, tracing a rectangular pattern through the sky. I climbed onto the picnic table to watch him land and as soon as he taxied in and shut down the engine, I ran out to hear about his adventure. After years of fencing our curiosity, Dad asked for Mom's approval to give us all flying lessons.

Mom finally agreed, but Dad had to make a couple promises.

First, we would only fly under a blue sky, avoiding any clouds. And second, we would only fly in a mechanically sound airplane. She wasn't fond of the idea of us flying a plane that had been taken apart and put back together in Dad's hangar. Dad may have the reputation of being an excellent mechanic, but he has some pretty hairy stories about flight-testing airplanes: trim wheels jamming, landing gear not coming down, and oil splattering the windshield so he had to land by looking out his side window. These were just a few of the tales passed around our dinner table when I was young. If it were up to me, I would rather fly an airplane after Dad finished his handiwork and gave it his sign of approval. Some of the junkers flying into the field would be better off as soda cans.

Tom and Dennis lost interest after their first couple of flight lessons, probably because they had already formed dreams and career plans beyond aviation, much to my mother's relief. Tom, my creative brother, has always been more interested in art and, now that he's pursuing a college degree, he has no time for flying.

Dennis, the outdoorsman, has been set on working for the Forest Service since I can remember. He is happily immersed in the Rocky Mountains, far from civilization. There just wasn't time in either of their busy schedules to add on flight lessons.

As for me, I can vividly recall the first lesson I had with my father. I was only eleven at the time, so it was really just an introduction. It was a hot summer afternoon and Dad was readying to pick up parts at an airport about fifty miles away. He told me to climb into the front seat, next to him. I couldn't see the ground over the instrument panel, so he found an old life preserver to act as a seat cushion. The airplane had a pale green interior and smelled a lot like Dad's mechanic shop. The familiar musty oil smell was seeping from the carpet.

Dad steered the airplane with his feet, but I could swear I was the one making it turn on the taxiway with the funny looking half wheel he called a yoke. He centered the nose on the runway and before long, I was staring out the side window, down at the green corn fields and farmhouses resembling some of my old toys.

Despite the cushion, it was difficult to see out the front of the plane. So Dad tapped a gauge on the panel in front of me and said, "Keep your eye on this." It was a circle with a little white line separating a blue-colored sky from a brown ground. In the center of the gauge was a miniature airplane. Dad advised me to keep the wings of the tiny airplane lined up on the white line representing the horizon. After I had managed to fly straight for a while, he told me to pull back on the yoke until the little plane was up in the blue and then push down until it was sinking into the brown half of the instrument. Dad laughed when I pushed forward. I must have done it pretty hard because my stomach dropped like it does on the rides at the county fair.

I had no fear that day. It was just pure excitement coursing through my body. Dad demonstrated how he would use his feet and hands together to turn the little airplane on the gauge. He would split its wings back and forth across the horizon line. To top it all off, when we landed at the new field, Dad introduced me to everyone as his little pilot. It was exhilarating. He even let me fly the whole way back home. I did it by watching the funny gauge most of the way as he moved the throttle.

Dad didn't really start teaching me until a couple years later, but I took to the lessons right away. Technically, I'm too young to be a student pilot, so Dad calls it "practice." For the entire month of June this year, we had one session a week. But by August, we were down to one lesson a month. Now he takes me up when he can get away from work, which is not very often.

The feeling of freedom and accomplishment the lessons give me is wonderful. I get more excited every time I see the horizon fall away.

The breeze grows stronger as I watch the last remaining patch of blue sky swallowed by a cluster of clouds. A thick, gray ceiling has begun to roll over the mountains, threatening the plains below. It's peaceful here watching the sky, so I delay climbing off the swing until the wind begins to swirl over the river. I figure I can make a run for the hangar if the rain really starts coming down.

Tiny droplets begin to pepper my bare arms as I hop off the swing and follow the path to a wide section of the river. I pause to watch a ladybug shuffle up a blade of grass and then lift away. The cattails are high and swaying back and forth. I tear one apart and watch it explode into a fluffy cotton firework to be carried away by the wind.

The buzz of an airplane engine overhead causes me to squint up at the sky and raise my hand to dispel the brightness of the rising cumulus clouds. Hmm, it's a yellow and white high winged plane and it looks an awful lot like the one Karl just bought. I guess Dad couldn't talk him out of flying it. I watch the airplane as it banks off to the east.

"I hope he makes it back alright," I whisper under my breath, remembering Dad's skepticism. Karl is as stubborn as anything and doesn't take to criticism or advice very well unless it agrees with his plans. He reminds me of a character from a movie, with his thick glasses and goofy sense of humor, interspersed with a heavy Scandinavian accent. Karl has been my father's best friend since high school. Really, he's like an uncle to my brothers and me. He was at both Tom and Dennis's graduation ceremonies. And he never forgets a birthday. But the main reason I like Karl so much is because he's the silliest adult I know.

Raindrops pelt my skin now, and I hear the sky grumbling its warnings to the ground below. I quicken my pace as a snake slithers across the path and into a patch of tall dandelions. The sudden movement makes me leap backwards, and I calm down when I realize it's a garden snake and not a rattler.

I pause to watch all the little critters as they dart into their hiding places amongst the weeds. Thunder slices my eardrums and I can tell the storm is much closer now. A beam of lightning awakens my senses and I run to reach the hangar before it unleashes its wrath on me. The downpour has begun.

I slip and slide in the softened earth trying to reach Dad's hangar door. As I push against the metal, I discover Dad's friends Dave and Jeff have taken Karl's place in conversation. The two men are sitting at the wooden picnic table outside Dad's office, munching on potato chips and laughing pretty hard at something I just missed.

"Well, look what the storm brought in. I didn't know you were out here today." Jeff pulls at his baseball cap and gestures over to the table, making room for me to sit down with them.

"Hey, Paul, do you have a towel to dry off this daughter of yours? She's soaked," Jeff says, smiling at the look on my face.

"Don't worry, this is a regular thing for her," Dad says, glancing sideways at my wet clothes. "I'd be surprised if she ever beat the storm to the hangar." He grins and nods his head in the direction of the bathroom. "If it wasn't for Grace, no one would ever use the bath towels in there anyway." Dad looks at me with amusement, and then buries his blackened hands inside the engine of a low-winged airplane.

I shiver and goose pimples dot my legs as I dry off in the bathroom. The hangar has cooled off and feels damp from the storm. I sit down on the bench next to Jeff and lay the towel across my thighs, noticing that my new sneakers are now covered in mud and grass stains. My mother bought them for me yesterday to wear to school and by the look on her face at the register, she was spending more than she could afford. I was spiteful when I put them on this morning, but now I feel guilty. Mom puts in extra hours at the local grocery store to help my brothers get through college and for me to have things for school, leaving her very little time for her artwork.

"Are you going to cook us up some s'mores at the picnic tonight?" Dave smiles, probably expecting me to shoot him a sarcastic answer. "You know, Eric and Brian are coming out in a little while with marshmallows and chocolate bars," he says, raising his eyebrows like this is fantastic news.

"Uh, I didn't know there was a picnic tonight...I think I have to finish school shopping with Mom," I answer, looking sheepishly at my father.

He frowns back at me, surely wondering how that is supposed to happen since Mom is working until well after the mall is closed.

Dad has to know that spending more than ten seconds with Dave's two sons is difficult for any girl my age. Eric is about a year older than I am, but, much to my discomfort, he's in the same class. I think Eric spent most of his sixth grade year in detention for all sorts of things like hiding snakes in desks, throwing grasshoppers at younger kids, chasing girls across the playground so he could pull their hair, and anything else that would draw attention to him.

Junior high school didn't tame Eric either; it just made him more of a bully. I remember the day he came hurtling toward me, caught a piece of my long hair in his hand and yanked hard. My only instinct was to turn and punch him as hard as I possibly could in the stomach. He gasped and his face went scarlet, but he really didn't bother me after that.

Brian, Eric's quiet younger brother, is much easier to handle. He has a sweeter disposition than Eric, and is more of the bookworm type. He keeps to himself mostly, and has a resigned temperament, evidence of relentless teasing from his older brother. If I have to spend the last day of summer break anywhere near Eric on the day that I'm supposed to be at the water park, it will definitely not go well.

"Well, Paul, if you want to stay tonight," Dave offers, "I'm sure Peggy could take Grace back to town after she drops off the boys. She wasn't planning on sticking around for the picnic."

"Thanks, Dave, we'll see. I'm so behind that I'll probably do as much as I can out here and then take Grace back to town. She got into a little trouble with her mom last night," he informs his friends as I cringe. "We shouldn't push our luck."

Dad goes back to loosening a screw and my mind wanders. I begin to think of how much fun my girlfriends must be having right now.

"Trouble?" Dave asks, smiling at me. "You never get in trouble, do you?"

"Well, it wasn't that big a deal...Dad, would you have been mad?"

"No comment, G," Dad replies, looking up from his work long enough for me to know that he doesn't want to talk about it either.

Dave brushes potato chip crumbs from his jeans. "Well, you must have done something really awful, Grace. Seems like your Dad's pretty upset." He's trying to provoke me and it's working.

41

"It was nothing, really," I object, crossing my arms. "My friends and I rode our bikes to the store and then stayed up late, looking at the stars."

This only encourages him. "Ohhh, were these friends boys?" he asks, raising his eyebrows.

"No, Dave, they were all girls. The same girls I'm supposed to be at the water park with right now." I walk to the bathroom to hang the towel back on the rack.

"Water park? Well, that's too bad. Now you're stuck with all of us old farts," Dave yells after me as he pops open a soda can.

I shoot him a half smile as I walk pass the men and head for the large hangar door, in need of a distraction from this exchange.

"Negotiations are getting ugly, Paul," Dave says, changing the subject and taking on a serious tone. "Jeff and I have already been out to the new field, sniffing out prices for a hangar rental. We figure if we're creative enough, we can fit two planes in one of the small hangars over there."

I look over my shoulder to see a shadow pass over Dad's countenance. "Really?" he asks. "What'd you find out?"

Dave shakes his head. "It's unbelievable what they're charging out there. I don't know how anyone can afford to own an airplane these days."

"At least you got a straight answer. Every time I step into that office, I get the feeling that Zack is telling the secretary to keep me at bay. I don't think he wants another shop to compete with," Dad says, hands covered in grease.

"I think you're right," Dave says. "Most of the pilots on that field go somewhere else for repairs. They say Zack has a hot temper and a thick wallet and has scared everyone away."

"That's the least of it," Jeff speaks up. "I hear he does shoddy work too. Mike took his Cherokee over there when you had a hangar full of planes. He said he'd never do that again."

"Humph." Dad doesn't look up.

Dave chimes in. "I'm just surprised that we can't get more support to keep this place open. I mean, Paul, this hangar alone has been here for sixty some years, hasn't it?"

Dad leans on the engine cowling that's propped up beside him. "Something like that. The problem is, the town is growing so fast and this is prime land, right next to the foothills. People don't see the importance of old airports like this. They have no idea that most pilots flying airliners got their wings at one of these dinky little fields. To the public, it's just a noisy waste of space. That's why we're probably the oldest airport in the state that hasn't been closed down or turned into a shopping center or parking lot. It's about money, not history." Dad's face is red and he's getting fired up.

Dave and Jeff both look resigned. Then Jeff stands up to admire the airplane that Dad is working on and remarks, "It's sad, that's all I can say."

"That's why we need to get together and try to fight for it, you know? We would be silly to give up and walk away," Dad says, gesturing with the wrench in his hand.

"Why don't we hold some fundraisers out here and put up a counter offer on the land?" Jeff asks.

"What kind of fundraiser is going to raise that kind of money though?" Dad frowns at Jeff.

"I don't know." Jeff shrugs. "Maybe Neil and some of his buddies can come out and put on a show in their shiny biplanes to get the ball rolling. We could grill some burgers and hot dogs and charge admission every Saturday."

Dad grins back at Jeff and then nods in my direction. "Grace had a similar idea. What we need are investors. But, I guess it's a start. Why don't you talk to Neil and see if he's interested?"

"Alright, Paul," Dave offers, "how about I call the guys and get everyone out here for that meeting so we can pick their brains for ideas, too. But," he continues, nodding at Jeff, "I like the idea of finding some investors. I thought all us guys who owned airplanes were supposed to be rich, anyway."

Jeff smirks at Dave and tosses his empty can into the bin for Dad to recycle.

"Thanks, Dave, I appreciate any help or time you guys can

give me," Dad says. "Ask everyone if they can meet an hour before Stonebrink shows up so we can come up with a plan." He points the wrench toward his office. "I have a list of phone numbers in there if you want to copy them down. I made it for Karl, but he decided to try and beat the storm out of here."

Dave gets off the bench and Dad ducks back into his work.

I turn to face the fresh air outside because I don't know what to say. I wish I could come up with something because I love this field too, but I don't understand how the deal making works. I just want to go and tell the development company to leave us alone and find some other land to build on. If I had thought of it, I'd have told Mr. Ted Skylar exactly what was on my mind.

I slide the main hangar door open a little wider and Jeff stands up from the table, giving me a reassuring pat on the shoulder as he passes by and heads out into the rain-kissed world. The storm has subsided a little, leaving the violet hint of a rainbow. I close my eyes and take a deep breath. I love how it smells during a summer storm, like the air and the earth have been washed clean. The vibrant colors draw me outside.

Chapter 7: A Visit With Betty

I step onto the pavement that leads from Dad's large hangar door to the parking ramp and notice that more thunderclouds are on the way. A wild rabbit hops around the weeds, nibbling on underbrush and watching me nervously. I get as close as I can, clicking my tongue at him until his white ball of a tail hops away into the thick weeds.

Passing by the main hangar, I attempt to count all the airplanes parked inside. It's amazing how many can fit into that space. On busy days, there are so many planes taxiing out of that hangar that I wonder if the owners don't stack them on top of each other when no one's looking.

Jeff is standing over a wide charcoal grill next to the building, struggling to light the coals inside. Whoosh! Suddenly, the entire thing is engulfed in flames as the smell of lighter fluid wafts through the air. He waves his hands through the smoke as I notice a car turning into the front parking area. I can see that Dave's wife, Peggy, is in the driver's seat. Her teased blonde hair is easy to spot. That can only mean his sons are in the car and now is the perfect time to go and visit Betty.

On my way to Betty, I notice that Henry's hangar door is cracked open. I squint my eyes, hoping to actually see into the darkness and to figure out what he does in there on days like today, but I cannot see a thing.

Betty's main door handle has been broken off for as long as I remember. Thankfully, Tom stowed a wrench next to the tail wheel to twist the bolt that holds the metal door in place. The door pops out as I turn the wrench, and the familiar smell of musty upholstery and wet papers wafts out.

"Wow," I say out loudly, overwhelmed by the scent of neglect. "I haven't been here for a while, I guess it's time to give you some fresh air, Betty."

Things look just as they did the last time I visited this old airplane, most likely seeking refuge from a thunderstorm then, too. Donated library books are stacked high in a corner, dampened from all the late summer storms. The beanbag Mom contributed to my little fort sits propped against old couch cushions in the rear of the plane. I slide it next to the door to allow the fresh air find its way through the cabin.

Curious as to what was left behind on my last visit, I hunch over to hike up the sloping floor and into the cockpit. My old journal lies in the torn left seat, water stained and faded by the sun. Droplets of rain pit patter on the floor through the window that I must have left ajar. Through the hazy glass I can see that dark clouds are building over the mountaintops again. I pick up the journal and thumb through its pages, hoping no one else noticed it lying here. Though my brothers haven't set foot in this airplane all summer, the thought of them reading my diary is more than disconcerting.

I slink lazily into the right seat, as it's much drier than the left. This cockpit offers the best vantage point for watching clouds spill over the mountains. After the downpour we just had, though, I'm surprised to see more weather on the way. Usually the storms are intense, but short lived.

I sit for a while and then pick up my journal, carrying it back to the soft, familiar seat below the rear window. The cushions crunch beneath my weight. I sit back and peer through the small, circular glass.

It would be nice to write about last night's meteor shower, but the pen that was tucked inside the journal won't even write a letter; it's dry as a stone. Instead, I stare out the window. The light is changing outside, illuminating the earth and sky with a purplish hue. Moisture lingers in the air. I trace circles in the mist that has formed on the window, as my eyes grow heavy with the quiet of the early evening and lack of sleep last night. I probably shouldn't stay in here too long.

Chapter 8: Buckle Up!

BAM! It feels like my head just hit the back end of a hammer. For a moment, all I can see is green and then blackness. My entire body is twisted and my stomach is wrenching like it does on a rough ride at the county fair and my surroundings are all out of focus.

Finally, a soft light reaches into the darkness and shadows begin to take shape around me.

There is a constant, deafening noise vibrating through the floor. It is almost unbearable as my head throbs with pain. It sounds as though I'm lying between two motorcycles, ceaselessly roaring their engines. I fight to get my bearings.

Grasping the back of my head with one hand and trying to push off the floor with the other, I'm quickly forced back onto the hard ground. Why is it so difficult to move? I lie for several seconds, dazed, until determination to wake up from this bizarre dream takes over.

I try again, propping myself on an elbow in an attempt to look around, to figure out where the heck I am. Holding onto a cold piece of metal, I pull my weight upward to see a dull gray light spilling through a tiny window, hardly illuminating the capsule I'm riding in. From the looks of it, the sun has gone down. It's difficult to tell for certain. I manage to pull myself up enough to peer outside the small, round glass. There's nothing but gray on the other side of the window, like I'm sitting in the middle of a cloud.

My left leg is asleep and stings sharply as I shift my weight, trying to regain my balance until a force pushes me flat on my belly again. Oh, no. A realization creeps over me like a cold draft of air. I'm in the back of an airplane...and it's flying!

The moments it takes to strain my head and look toward the cockpit feel like hours. I am facing the unknown. I have no idea how I got here or who might be at the controls.

A soft light emanates from the front of the airplane and I

can see familiar round gauges staring back at me. There is a figure occupying the left seat, but no one on the right. Could it be Karl? Did Dad actually let me fly with Karl? My mind is racing and I feel disoriented. I've heard about kids being kidnapped, but surely I would remember something about it. Could I really still be drowsing away and this is just a vivid dream?

I sit as still as the airplane allows me to, but my heart is racing. What do I do? I have to formulate a plan. But first, I must assess the space around me. Forms are coming in clearer every second. The man in the left seat has long, wavy hair poking out around a pair of headphones and his hand is manipulating the many levers in the center of the cockpit. It's the smallest hand I've ever seen on a man. Hm. If he's small, then I may just be able to manage to escape as soon as the airplane is on the ground. That's it. It'll be dark soon, so as soon as we roll to a stop, I'll open the door and jump out, and run as fast as I can into the night.

The fear that was stifling my movements is overtaken by a curiosity to see inside the cockpit. I need to evaluate the situation. The longer it takes me to move forward, the longer I am able to look around the cabin, and it seems uncannily familiar. The area is fairly small and the walls are covered in fine upholstery. The seats before me are empty and I can see the metal rail that I bumped the back of my head on. Where have I seen this plane before?

I finally build enough strength and balance to pull myself off the floor and work my way to the cockpit, holding onto seat corners. My legs are wobbling as the airplane rises and falls like a ship lost at sea. I can't tell if the noise is from the engines or the thunderclouds outside the window, but it is raucous.

The next bump sends me into one of the seats, right on top of a leather jacket. Its zipper digs into my leg and as I yank it out from beneath me, I feel its smooth material. It looks like a coat my father wears when he works outside in the winter, awfully heavy for this time of year. There is a name that I cannot read patched onto the front of it. The letters are too faded for this light, but I can make out a small figure with wings sewn above the left pocket.

I lean as far forward as I can to look inside the cockpit without falling out of the seat. The man must have a smaller frame than I had thought, because I can't even see his shoulders. I strain my neck to see a smooth jaw line and neatly curled hair.

Is it a woman? I don't know any females that fly out of my Dad's field. I'm staring so long that my neck muscles begin to cramp and a patch of rough air sends me onto my knees at the front of the cabin. The movement must have caught the pilot's eye, for she turns and meets my gaze with a look of horror. She flinches in her seat and then shouts something inaudible over the engines. Her right hand, which had risen to her chest, is now brushing back the wisps of hair around her face so she can get a better look at me.

The woman has high cheekbones and wide eyes that are searching mine. Her hair is waved away from her forehead and I can see the bobby pins that hold it off her face. She looks vaguely familiar, like someone I've seen in a movie or magazine. The two of us stare at each other for a few moments until the turbulence returns, taking her focus back to the task at hand. She looks perturbed as her eyes trace the instruments and then glance outside. It seems as though my presence disturbs her.

I watch the pilot, realizing this couldn't possibly be a kidnapping; otherwise why would she be so shocked to see my face? She clearly didn't know I was here, unless I was knocked out and she didn't expect me to wake up.

After what feels like an hour, the woman pulls the right side of her headphones off and shouts to me over the rumble, "Dear, are you a runaway?" Her eyes look so deeply into mine that I'm compelled to look away, like I've just been caught doing something terribly wrong.

I shake my head, grasping for a response. "No. I...well...I think I must have fallen asleep or something."

The woman cups a hand over her ear like she's having

trouble hearing me, and then shouts, "I looked this plane over inside and out before I left Hondo. Where could you possibly have hidden yourself?"

She is demanding an answer and I have none. I think hard, desperately trying to recall where I was prior to standing next to this woman flying the airplane. I remember the thunder and Jeff lighting the charcoal grill, and then climbing into Beached Betty. Wait a minute. Did she say Hondo? Is Hondo an airport or a town?

The pilot frowns at the darkening sky and then taps the seat next to her. "Well, you'd better take a seat, buckle up, and help me navigate around these darned thunderstorms. The fuel gauges haven't been reading properly since I left and now I'm afraid we won't make it to Casper. We need to get on the ground."

I feel her watching me closely as I maneuver into the right seat. I sink low into the metal frame, as there is no cushion on the seat. I take off my sweatshirt and fold it up beneath me, but the air gives me a chill. I shiver as I stare at the instruments. I've seen these before. The pointer with the ball underneath, the circular compass, even the miniature airplane gauge is familiar, but cruder than the ones in my father's plane.

The woman tugs at a strap behind my shoulder, indicating that I should fasten the seat belt. It takes a while to figure out how it works, but I get it buckled as the airplane bounces through the sky.

The yoke in front of me is adorned with a silver B, and has been polished to a high shine. There are several levers in between the pilot and I and the woman is periodically adjusting them. Each lever has a letter stamped into its handle, but I cannot figure out what they mean, or why there are so many. What could they possibly all be used for? Dad's plane only has three.

The entire cockpit looks as though someone has spent a great deal of time restoring it to its original state. Dad would be very impressed. If I can find my way home, I'll show it to him.

"This plane is in great shape!" I shout.

The woman looks questioningly at me. "It looks a lot better than it did a month ago, I'm certain of that! It didn't even have seats in the back the last time I flew it."

I look out the front windows, attempting to discern where we are, but there are dark clouds all around us. The pilot is trying to maneuver between two of them as we get swallowed in the middle. All I see is grey for several seconds, then flashes of ground far beneath us. When we come out of the cloud, wispy streams of moisture lie ahead, strewn from a cluster above us. The streams resemble thin cotton candy as it's wrapped around a paper cone.

Suddenly it feels like we are dropping out of the sky. The airplane is rocking and descending as the woman brings the middle levers forward and traces her eyes over the instruments. She pulls on the yoke and from the crude version of Dad's airplane gauge, it looks like we're climbing again. An unseen force shakes the entire airplane.

If the woman is bothered by the turbulence, she certainly doesn't show it. Rather, it appears to be a nuisance as she keeps working to keep the wings level. But the bumps grow more intense. I watch as she jockeys the levers with her right hand and tightens her grip on the yoke with her left. The woman methodically moves a couple of levers, turns the black wheel next to her seat slightly, and then lifts her right hand to rotate a handle above her head. All the while, her eyes dart between the instruments and the sky beyond the cockpit. I watch her, transfixed by the certainty of her movements, until she turns and shouts at me again.

"What's your name?" she asks.

"Grace!" I shout back, choking over the sound of my own voice.

"I'm Dorothy!" The woman smiles politely and I watch her eyes shift back to the instruments, then outside again. "It looks like we're ending in Cheyenne tonight because it'll be too dark to make it to Casper. We'll have to RON there and then figure out what to do with you in the morning. I'm sure your parents are awfully upset about this!" She shouts over the

51

engines.

Ron in Cheyenne? What the heck is she talking about? It's like the woman is speaking a different language. "It would take an hour to fly to Cheyenne and back tonight, I have to get home!" I shout back. Besides, tomorrow is the first day back to school...not that I would mind missing it for this.

Dorothy reaches behind my seat and sets a pair of headphones into my lap, just like the ones she's wearing. Pointing to where I should plug them in she shouts, "I don't have a parachute for you, either!"

I'm not jumping out of this thing! I pull the leather headphones over my ears, anticipating them to silence some of the noise, but they don't. It's so cold in here my teeth are clicking together and my body is shuddering. I reconsider the sweatshirt beneath me and as I start to lift it out of the seat, Dorothy points to the jacket in the back.

"Go put on my leather coat or you'll catch your death from cold!" Dorothy takes the headphones from me as I climb in back to retrieve the jacket.

It's the heaviest coat I've ever worn, but the leather is wonderfully soft and the inside is like the sheepskin rug my mother used to have. I'm thankful for the warmth.

The two of us sit quietly as I notice the horizon has nearly faded into darkness. We silently bump in and out of clouds. I have no idea how I got here, but right now I don't care. The last hint of sunset filters through the moist air, lighting the cockpit with a lavender glow. My fear melts away for a moment, and I suddenly realize how beautiful it is to be flying right now.

"I was supposed to land about fifty miles back, in Denver," Dorothy's voice carries through my headphones. I look over and she's holding an object up to her mouth and speaking through it. It must be a microphone like the one Dad never uses in his plane.

"I had a fuel stop scheduled, but I couldn't get in to the field!" Dorothy's eyes search my face for an expression. "Boy, I've skirted around a thunderstorm or two before, but this is the worst I have ever seen. I had to abort the landing three times because the wind changed so much and I didn't have enough rudder to keep it straight, even with power. On the third try, dust started kicking up at the end of the runway, and I knew it was time to get out of there!" she says, looking straight ahead.

Dorothy doesn't need to explain her reasoning to me. Too many times, Dad has come home with stories about airplanes trying to race a thunderstorm back to the airfield. The airplanes rarely won. I remember one story of a pilot who tried to force a landing in an obscene crosswind. He made it onto the ground, but the wind lifted the airplane's upwind wing and flipped it onto its back like a piece of cardboard. Luckily, the pilot and his passenger were able to walk away from the crash, but many stories did not end as well.

"I tried to turn around, but the storm came in quickly over the mountains and I...well, WE, were surrounded. Had I known you were on board, I would have landed in a field. I should have done that anyway, because now we're in the thick of it." Dorothy is clearly burdened by my presence. But I hadn't asked to be taken on this adventure of dodging thunderstorms with dwindling fuel. Besides, I can only imagine what my father will say when I finally make it back to the airport...if I ever do.

The thought makes me desperate to find somewhat level ground beneath the clouds for us to land on. I tilt my head against the side window and search for a familiar mountain range or road or river below, anything to possibly clue me in to our location. But it's getting very difficult to see now.

The airplane begins to rock back and forth again. Rain pounds the windshield and I watch Dorothy fight to keep it steady. I think of my mom and her last flight with my father; how she must have felt as they dodged thunderstorms together. The airplane seems to be out of control, rising and falling and rocking as though it was a toy, caught in a giant's hand.

I look at Dorothy and all I see is the outline of her profile as a burst of lightning showers the cockpit. I close my eyes to dispel the temporary blindness, but it doesn't work. In the eerie moments it takes me to adjust to the dim cockpit again, I attempt to shake off the fear as it works its way into my limbs until my entire body is trembling. I try to calm down by telling myself that we will make it back to my Dad, we will get on the ground safely. When I regain my sight, I look over at Dorothy and she is fiddling with the lights over the instrument panel. The resolve I feel is reflected in her face. It makes me feel strong.

Then bullets hit. Or what sounds like bullets. We are either being pounded by hail or someone is hurling boulders at the metal airframe. I'm guessing it's the former, because I can see a thick slush building on the corners of the windows outside.

Dorothy pulls back on the yoke, probably trying to climb us out of this mess. But the airplane is sluggish and not wanting to climb at all. She flips some switches and maneuvers the airplane as I watch her, feeling helpless.

Dorothy studies the chart in her lap and I figure she must be giving up on the climb, because now she's letting the airplane descend. The hammering of the hail slows and, in a few breathless moments, it dissipates. The steady pounding of rain hitting the windshield takes over.

I saw foothills beneath us earlier, so I'm well aware that a descent into these clouds could be deadly. I shout over the engines because I'm too impatient to figure out how to use the microphone. "Do you know where we are?"

Dorothy points to a map that looks like it's pinned to her pant leg, "South of Cheyenne. I was paralleling the road here, but now it's dark and my compass is bouncing every which way. I think I made too much of a wind correction and brought us over the foothills here to the southwest."

I lean over the center console to see where her slender finger is tapping, but the map looks like nothing I've seen before. There are lines and letters, scribbled notes with arrows. It reminds me of a treasure map my brothers used to carry around.

Dorothy strains to see something ahead of us and then checks the compass above the instruments. "My plan was not to land in a field. This airplane has to make it to Casper and then on to some General out in California. And let me tell you, I flew it before they spruced it up like this. It's a whole new airplane now." Dorothy frowns. "And I just cannot stand the idea of nosing it over in the mud on some farmer's field. I wanted to deliver it without even a speck of dirt. But if we fly much longer, I won't have a choice." She puts down the microphone, but her lips are still moving; the drone of the engines usurps all sound.

Dorothy is solemn for a few minutes. I imagine she has to rest after brawling with the airplane and the turbulence. Finally, she picks up the microphone. "I need you to do something for me." She studies my face again and I notice her eyes are an intense, deep blue, bordered by long, curled lashes.

I nod. "Do you want me to fly for a while?" I ask with excitement building in my chest.

Dorothy looks surprised at this, but smiles kindly. "Some other time, dear. I don't want to take any more chances by trying to get to Cheyenne. There's an airfield right here, but I've lost the beam because we're too far out." She looks at me and points back to the map. "I need you to help me look for the field before we run out of light or fuel trying to get around these storms. I'd rather put it down there than hope for some farmer to find us tomorrow morning." She manages a smile and slides the map toward me.

I don't like the idea of landing in darkness in a field either. What if we hit a house or someone's barn instead? What about the power lines Dad and Karl were talking about?

I look at the map in the soft lights coming from above the instruments, but it might as well be written in a different language, so I go back to scouring signs of ground instead. I can see just enough to follow the slope of the land. It looks like we're flying over the foothills, but nothing looks even remotely safe for a landing.

"We should be about ten miles away," Dorothy says, just as the clouds envelope us again. "I don't know why they didn't fix this darned radio!"

"If this area is Cheyenne," I say, pointing to the treasure map, "then my Dad has a repair shop on an airfield not far from here."

"Golly, I'll bet it's the field I'm looking for! Does your Dad work for the military?" Dorothy sits upright.

I shake my head. "No." What a strange question. The nearest military facility is in Cheyenne, but I suppose Dorothy doesn't know this area.

"Dad has his own shop," I explain. "It used to be a public airfield, but now you have to get permission to land there." I shrug. "But no one really does."

"Well, my dear, I say we have permission." Dorothy smiles for real now. "I'd sure like your dad to look at these fuel gauges, too. We should have more than this." Dorothy points at a small round gauge and then peers over me, trying to see out my side window.

I watch as the woman turns knobs on an archaic looking device mounted above my head. She leans forward and presses her hand against her headphones, as if she is straining to hear something. Dorothy's dance with all the levers and handles now includes turning dials on the black box mounted above my head. Her eyes and hands never stop moving. I watch her move one of the smaller levers slightly as she stares out her side window at the engine. Leaning back to see what she is looking at, I spot a flame coming from the side of the engine!

"Is it on fire?" I shout with panic in my voice.

"Exhaust," she says, shaking her head. "I'm trying to save our fuel."

I look beyond Dorothy and notice a familiar rise of foothills on the left side of the airplane. I recognize the outline of the hills as the ones Dad flies next to on our "lake tour," as he calls it.

"Wait, I recognize this these hills!" I lean toward Dorothy and press my face close to the windshield.

Dorothy follows my searching eyes and looks out her side window. "Can you see any flat ground on your side?"

I can see a couple lights, perhaps homes set against the

hillside. I strain to see more, to remember exactly where we are. There's an outline of trees topping a hill and a rugged rock formation I have seen many times before. "No, but the airport isn't far!" I finally shout back. "This line of foothills is connected by a couple of dams," I say, pointing ahead to the left of the airplane.

Dorothy is shaking her head and motioning to her headset. She signals to the microphone on my side of the plane, and moves her thumb, indicating how to use it.

I lift the brown handle from its holder and push the button on the side. "If we stay on this track, next to the foothills, we'll eventually pass a few dams. The third dam has a red and white painted water tower just beneath it and the airfield is really close to the water tower!"

Dorothy uses her own microphone. "It must be the field on my chart! We just passed a dam, but I didn't see a water tower." She searches my face.

"It's the last one! It should be just in front of us! I'll keep watching out your side to make sure we're on track." Dorothy nods in agreement and I take a deep breath. I feel like there is hope, although I'm beginning to really enjoy this flying escapade. Dorothy doesn't seem to be phased by anything. She's calm and confident, but I can't tell if fear is hiding beneath her soft exterior. Maybe she's trying to keep me at ease.

Dorothy gives one of the gauges she's been staring a hard tap, frowning at its position. "We are nearly out of fuel. I'll fly ten miles north and we can keep our eyes peeled for the tower. If you see it, let me know so I can circle and start down. If neither of us spots it, I'll turn around and descend a thousand feet so we can get a closer look. But I can't get any lower than that unless we head east." She is talking through the microphone and leaning to see out the window on her side.

I give the thumbs up sign and my stomach tightens as the lights on the ground begin to blur. They disappear and we're back in the clouds. Did she say we're nearly out of fuel as well? That's not reassuring.

The airplane feels like it's falling and I'm weightless for a moment. The bumps are back. Though Dorothy's movements are quick, she seems at ease with the situation, like it's just another day. She lets the plane maneuver the bumps. I notice Dorothy has stopped listening to the sounds over the radio, too. Either she finally heard what she was searching for or she has given up. Now her focus is outside the airplane.

My stomach drops to my knees as it feels like we're on a roller coaster ride again, and this time it's pointed toward the ground. Dorothy pushes two levers forward smoothly and raises the nose of the airplane. I see that the gauge she was tapping earlier is now pegged at the bottom and we are rising fast. Fear creeps under my skin. I look at Dorothy and I swear that, for a second, I can see panic in her face as well, but it is quickly replaced by determination. For the next few minutes, she struggles with the airplane the best she can, trying to keep the wings level. Again, the airplane feels like it's falling from the sky. There's a flash of light on the ground ahead of us and I look at the spot, waiting for it to flash again.

Is Dorothy deliberately descending? She must have seen the flash of light too.

"Beacon!" Dorothy is pointing. "Beacon, I just saw it flash!"

I look at the space where her finger is pointing, but all I can see is a white layer of fog with some haze beneath.

"It's all right, we just have to get a little lower," Dorothy says calmly as I frantically search for the airfield.

And then, just as she tilts the nose a bit lower, I see it! The old dam near our airstrip! I point, unable to speak over my relief. But then I see a layer of white beneath the dam and just the tip of the water tower is visible. The beacon is apparently right in the center of the white, as I can barely see it, flashing through the haze. I didn't realize they even had a light right there. I guess I've never flown into this field at night.

It must be moonlight illuminating the road across the dam, because I can see the stony wall that links the foothills together. Could that be the moon already? Without it, we wouldn't have been able to see anything except the blur of lights on the ground. There is a blaze emanating from the airstrip, but it's difficult to see where the runway might be.

"I see the lights, but it may be too fogged in to see the runway clearly!" Dorothy yanks at my seat belt to make sure it's secure and then points the nose down toward the space where the landing strip should be. The hail subsided several minutes ago, but the visibility is terrible. At the moment, I'd take the hail over this. It's impossible to discern anything below or ahead of us. And just when I begin to see clearly, the lights blend into a deep glow.

Suddenly the airplane lurches hard to the left and it feels like we hit the ground. Dorothy's left leg is pressed to the floor, trying to straighten us, but it feels like I'm leaning sideways in my seat. She pushes a red button on the panel and moves the levers all so quickly but the silence speaks for both of us. One of the engines has quit. We are going down, and I can feel her battling the airplane, fighting to keep us flying.

"There!" I point to the lights just off to our left. It looks like someone has lit fires all along the edge of the runway. Dorothy reacts quickly, struggling to point the nose of the plane in the direction of the lights. We are losing altitude a lot quicker than I'm comfortable with.

"Hold on!" Dorothy shouts.

Chapter 9: Only a Dream?

I wake up curled over something that feels like the handlebars from my bicycle. My head is aching and water is dripping slowly into my eye. Something hard and cold as stone is pressing into my chest and it's difficult to move.

"Grace!"

"Dad?" I raise my head and feel around me for something to push against in order to sit up. Lights flash ahead in the distance.

"Grace, honey, are you alright? Wake up!"

Was I sleeping? Was I dreaming? Someone is pointing a bright light into my eyes which makes my head throb with my pulse.

"Grace, what the hell happened to you? What are you doing in there?" I can hear Dad's voice, but he is hidden somewhere behind the light. Then I feel a hand against my forehead.

"You're bleeding! Oh, G, what happened?" Dad asks and then shouts, "I've found her! Can I get another light in here?"

I can see Dad's eyes now. They look wild, searching my face. He leans forward to grab me, but something is constraining my body.

"Why is your seat belt on, Grace? Why in the hell are you hiding in here? Didn't you hear Karl land?"

The seat next to me is empty. "Where is Dorothy, Dad? Is she okay?"

He isn't listening to me. I hear another voice and suddenly the entire cockpit is illuminated. I cover my eyes and feel the wetness on my forehead and look down at my hand to find blood, dark red blood. Suddenly, I feel queasy. Why is my forehead bleeding like never before?

"We can get her out if you like. Is she stuck?" The voice is unfamiliar.

Then I hear my Dad reply, "No, just leave the light on so I

can see her. I should be able to get her out..." my Dad's voice is getting softer. He is talking to someone outside.

I hear objects being shifted around somewhere behind me, and then footsteps move closer.

"She must have been out cold to miss all the noise around here," says the man.

Dad is next to me again and I feel him tugging at the seat belt, but it just falls away. The shredded material collapses into my lap. The buckle must have fallen off.

"Come on, G." He wraps one arm around my shoulder and the other beneath my knee. Just as he lifts me out of the seat, I feel something fall from my leg onto the floor.

"Wait, Dad!" I reach down, running my hand over the dirt and grime on the floor beneath me.

"I'll get it tomorrow, Grace...whatever it is. We have to get you out of here, it's cold and you're still soaking wet."

Finally, my hand finds something soft, like a piece of material. I quickly shove it into my pocket as Dad carries me out of the airplane.

The fire department has taken over my father's hangar. The fireman who helped Dad get me out of the airplane placed a blanket around my shoulders and now I'm sitting on the picnic table, taking everything in.

There are people milling about everywhere. Most of them are local firefighters and I rarely see them out on the field, but some of the other faces I recognize as regulars. I cannot figure out what all the commotion is about. Firemen don't usually go to picnics dressed in their big, yellow suits, do they? And everyone is very serious. Even Dad is standing in front of me, giving me the third degree, though I can't really pay attention to what he's saying.

Thankfully, a woman wearing a blue uniform steps in front of my dad, interrupting him to clean the cut on my forehead. She waves a flashlight in front of my eyes and I am immeasurably grateful when she tells him I don't need stitches. Relief passes over Dad's face and he folds his arms across his chest to peruse the scene in his hangar, as though he has just become aware of the madness around him.

After running his hands through his hair several times and answering a few questions from the woman who nursed my head, Dad reluctantly heads into his office and picks up the telephone. I don't have to ask whom he is calling at this hour. It's obviously Mom. She'll give him an earful when he explains what happened.

I look to the corner of the hangar and notice Karl, talking and gesturing to a small audience gathered around him. He looks like he's seen a ghost.

A local police officer named Sam, who often stops by to check on the airport, hovers on one side of Karl, and the manager of the airport stands attentive at his other side. They are both listening to every word Karl says and nodding occasionally. No one is laughing.

A tall, gray-haired man wearing khaki pants and a polo shirt is listening to Karl and writing notes on a clipboard. I move closer to hear the conversation.

"On the sixth or seventh attempt, I knew I just had to land it on its belly," Karl says, looking wildly at his spectators. "I was lucky, that's all I can say. The fog was getting thicker and thicker...I could barely see even the roads leading up to the airport..."

"Come on, Grace, I'm taking you to your mom's house," Dad says, suddenly blocking my view of the scene.

"Dad, wait, what happened to Karl?" I'm not about to leave, not when things are so exciting.

"It's a long story, Grace. I'll tell you on the way." Dad tries to smile, but his eyes are weary from stress.

"But, Dad, you can't possibly leave with all these people in your hangar," I say, hoping to delay the inevitable.

"Yes I can, G. I'm coming back. You, on the other hand, are going to your mom's house. You have school tomorrow and your mother is about to take away my privileges of seeing you." He struggles over the last sentence. "Please, Grace, we really have to go."

As I grudgingly follow Dad out to his old pickup truck, I

glance across the alley toward the entrance of the main hangar. A floodlight spills onto the metal door and I notice a man standing in the shadows thrown by the light, watching us climb into the truck. It's a man with white hair. It's Henry. Dad follows my gaze to the old man, but doesn't seem to be bothered by him standing there, motionless. I can feel his icy blue eyes staring through me. I shift in my seat and Dad must notice how uncomfortable I am because he acknowledges the old man with a friendly wave.

"Good evening," Dad says to Henry as we pass by him slowly.

The old man still doesn't respond. In the shadowy light, his eyes look black as he studies me and his frown deepens as we drive by. It's like he doesn't even notice my father.

"Everything alright, Henry?" Dad slows the truck.

The old man finally acknowledges Dad with a nod, looks at me one last time, and then walks off toward his hangar.

"That was strange," Dad says, looking at me.

"Uh, yeah. Did you see how he was staring at me?" I ask. "He's really creepy, Dad. One time, I saw him outside his hangar, wandering around, talking to himself."

Dad laughs. "I wander around talking to myself too, G, does that make me creepy?"

"Yes!" I exclaim, giggling.

I can see the stress fade from his forehead.

"Dad, what happened to Karl?" I ask again, hoping to change the subject, but not push my father into total silence.

"Oh, G, I don't even know where to begin." He shakes his head and turns onto the paved road, heading back into town.

It's a while before Dad speaks again. He just slouches forward, clutching the steering wheel like there's a weight resting on his shoulders. "Karl just doesn't think sometimes, Grace."

I stay quiet so Dad will keep talking, but all I can think of is Dorothy. How could I have had a dream that was so real? Then again, Betty is in no shape to fly and I was really tired when I climbed inside the old plane to give her some air.

"He flew that damned broken airplane to Nebraska, knowing there were thunderstorms coming in," Dad breaks my concentration and slows the truck down so much I could walk to Mom's house from here and still beat him. He turns the corner and I see Mom has left her porch light on.

"Then he tried to land the plane in the fog, with landing gear that wouldn't come down. It could have been much worse and that's what worries me." I watch Dad shake the last cigarette out of a pack and crush the empty box in his palm. "He was lucky this time, G. Karl is the just about the luckiest guy I know."

I don't remember my father ever being angry with Karl. They can bicker back and forth for hours, but they always seem to be laughing on the inside. "So, is he alright, Dad? I mean is he going to be in trouble?"

Dad pulls over and stares ahead at the space between the streetlights. He shakes his head. "Well, you know Karl. That guy can talk his way out of just about anything. Maybe he can talk his way out of this."

"Who were all those men standing around him?" I ask.

"Oh, just people who have to get his version of what happened...some of them were just being nosy. But he'll have to fill out an accident report, that's for sure." Dad looks me like he's seeing my face for the first time. He is looking at the cut on my forehead that I had forgotten about.

"What am I going to do with you, Grace? How am I going to keep you safe out at that silly airport if this is what happens when you supposedly doze off?" He asks, examining the bandage over my eyebrow. "You know, if Karl hadn't caused so much commotion tonight, I would have really panicked...I didn't realize that you weren't at the picnic until the firefighters showed up."

I don't like this change of subject and I especially don't like having to defend myself for simply falling asleep. "I'm sorry, Dad. I guess I was just really tired from staying up late last night. I must have been out before the picnic even started."

"Grace," Dad says, leaning close to my face so his green

eyes are illuminated by the streetlights. I can tell he's assessing the bandage on my forehead. "Come on. I know your mother as well as you do." He leans away and sighs. "You had better think of a better excuse for her, or I won't be able to see you for a long time." His tone is serious. "I'm not kidding, Grace. How do you cut your forehead while you're asleep?"

"Maybe it was the tree branch from when I was swinging, Dad," I say, convincing myself as well. "I promise I don't know how it happened. And I didn't miss the picnic on purpose. I wasn't trying to make you angry. I wanted to hang out inside the airplane because I didn't want to see Eric. I can't stand that kid!" I'm grasping for explanations because I don't understand it myself. So I switch the discussion back to Karl. "What did Karl mean by making six or seven attempts?"

"Six or seven attempts? Oh. I guess he tried to cycle the landing gear several times," Dad answers, running his hand through his hair and rolling the cigarette between his fingers. He plugs in the lighter. "Obviously it didn't come down, just like I warned him."

"Hmm, so did he land in a field, like you said he would have to?" I ask.

Dad frowns at me. "No G, he scraped it onto the runway a hundred yards from where you were supposedly knocked out...right after he announced over the radio he was making an emergency landing."

"Is that why the firefighters came out?" I ask.

"Well, I think Jeff heard Karl's radio calls from inside the office. He asked Karl if he needed help and when Karl didn't respond, well, Jeff called it in. I mean, the station is right next door, so it doesn't take very long." Dad sits, shaking his head. "But he said something strange to the investigators and I really wish he hadn't."

"Karl did?" I ask.

Dad looks up at the streetlight. "The fog had rolled in, and none of us really noticed it for a while because we were eating inside the hangar. Anyway, one of the firefighters came in and asked how to radio the airplane that was having trouble outside.

When I went out, all I could think of was where you were. I got really worried and started looking everywhere," Dad explains.

I try to interrupt, but he raises his hand to stop me.

"I didn't think to check the old airplane at first. I grabbed a flashlight and started out to the tree you like to visit instead. At least that's where I tried to go. I had to give up because I couldn't see five feet in front of me." Dad lights the cigarette from the car lighter.

"Then I heard an airplane overhead, and it was really loud, like it was circling or something. I figured whoever it was, they would realize how bad the visibility was and divert somewhere else. But the next thing I know, Karl is landing his airplane with the gear up, screeching and scraping metal down the runway and the whole darned fire department is howling around the corner."

"So, Karl landed on the runway? How could he see it in the fog?" I ask, suddenly remembering the dream I had and how Dorothy and I couldn't see the runway until the last moment.

We are still parked a few houses down from Mom's place and I can see Dad's face clearly in the moonlight. He turns to me and says, "I know he's shaken up, but Karl said that the only way he could see the airport was to follow the airplane in front of him."

"You mean, like, he saw another airplane flying tonight? Who, Dad? Who else landed in the fog?"

"No one," Dad answers, throwing up his hand. "I was outside the entire time. I was looking for you." He scratches his forehead. "The plane I heard sounded louder than Karl's, and the engines didn't sound right. I thought it was in trouble, but it certainly didn't land. There were other people out there. We would have seen it."

I stare at the mailbox in front of Mom's house and her overflowing flower box. So many petals have fallen to the ground, dusting the grass with deep red highlights.

An eerie feeling creeps over me. "Did Karl say what the airplane looked like?" I ask.

"I don't know...I'm sure he didn't, between the darkness and the fog. I'm betting he barely saw the runway." Dad looks defeated. "But I am worried about how it all this sounds to the investigators. Hell, maybe Karl should have his license taken away. It'd be a relief to me."

I ignore Dad's last words. "Why would Karl make something like that up, Dad? You even said that you heard a plane that didn't sound like Karl's. Maybe someone was trying to land to get out of the thunderstorm and then they decided not to at the last minute."

"Grace, I would have heard them! I wasn't that far from the runway," he says, putting the truck in gear and driving forward to park in front of Mom's house.

"Hmm. Dad," I start a sentence without thinking. He looks at me and I can see how exhausted he is. "That's so weird that Karl landed in the fog when that was just like the dream I had. I dreamt I was flying with this lady…"

"Grace," Dad interrupts me, "your mom's at the door. Why don't we talk about this later?"

"Oh." I sit, shaken by nerves that have been building since I woke up. Mom waves to me from her screen door. I wave back absentmindedly.

"You ok, Grace?" Dad asks with a worried look.

"Sure," I answer, climbing out of the truck. "I'll see you next weekend, Dad."

He says goodbye before I let the door slam. The only way to close it is to slam it, I have learned. As I walk up the sidewalk, Mom's figure moves away from the glass door. I'm sure she has been pacing the floor, waiting for me for hours now. She must be too mad at my father to even acknowledge him.

I stuff my hands into the front pocket of my shorts and feel something soft rub against my palm. I had forgotten about the object that I'd strained to retrieve off the floor of the plane before Dad carried me out.

I pull the soft fabric out of my pocket. It's a large round patch that looks like a cartoon image of a girl with flying goggles and wings.

My heart drops when I read the name sewn into it. Dorothy Morrow? It's the patch from Dorothy's leather jacket!

Chapter 10: Freedom

The wind feels good against my face. I balance myself on my bicycle pedals and glide over the ground, closing my eyes for a second. It's the first time I have ridden my bike in almost a month.

The sun warms my skin and it's one of those temperate autumn days, indicative of a summer that has been recently laid to rest. I ride next to the curb where the trees block the sunlight. The air is cooler in the shadows, much cooler than the last time I rode to my friend Sunny's house, just days before my adventure at the airfield.

Dad was right; my mom was livid when he dropped me off at her house two hours late, sporting a nasty cut above my eyebrow. Even now, she blames my disappearance on my father. She said it never would have happened if he had been paying attention to me.

Needless to say, I was grounded from the airport and my bicycle and really anything fun for the past month because I wouldn't tell Mom what happened. How could I? I mean, if I had told her everything, she would have sent me to the school psychologist.

Mom even switched her schedule at the grocery store so that she could be home on the weekends with me. Dad didn't like the arrangement, but he wouldn't argue with my feisty mother. He knew there wasn't much he could do about it.

I round the corner of Sunny's block and almost pummel a boy balancing on his skateboard. He flashes me a nasty gesture and I'm tempted to slam on my brakes and send him to the moon, but I continue on. Besides, he looks like one of my friend's younger brothers. And I certainly don't need an episode that would get me in trouble all over again.

My lungs burn as I pedal harder and take in as much air as possible, thinking that this past month wasn't a total loss. I did discover that when Mom can't sleep, she pours a glass of wine and takes it out to her garage, dons her sculpting apron, and begins to "rock out," as I call it.

It was after midnight on the Friday after I was grounded when I found out what Mom was up to. I was having trouble sleeping so I went to lie down on the couch and watch TV. It sounded like a freight train was rolling over the roof. When I went out to the garage to investigate, there was Mom, standing beneath a bright light clamped to some shelving above her head. She was holding a massive saw and cutting through a slab of marble, with tiny particles flying everywhere. She leapt backward and nearly dropped the saw when she noticed me standing in the doorway in my pajamas.

Now Mom lets me join her in the garage when I can't sleep. As long as it's not a school night, she lets me be a night owl. And I have to admit; it is cool to witness her transformation from strict disciplinarian to powerfully creative artist, focused on whatever stone she is shaping. Mom works until a sheet of dust covers every corner of the garage, cutting through marble with a saw, carving graceful lines into alabaster with all sorts of metal files, and sanding rough stone until it's as smooth as glass. By the time she's finished, her knuckles are swollen and the skin is cracked and bleeding, but Mom never gives up on her stone. Within weeks, a giant block of jagged marble becomes a flowering vine, flanked with streaks of green that naturally occur throughout the stone.

For the first time in a while, Mom and I actually had fun together, which is nice because we haven't been getting along very well over the last few years. She doesn't understand my need for independence and I don't get why she's so protective. But our nights together in her garage remind me of when I was really young, when Mom would prop up a piece of canvas stapled to wood and then give me a handful of paintbrushes and let me paint to my heart's content. Last night I managed to turn a coarse rock into the shape of a lopsided doorknob. Not very impressive to most, but I was proud.

I finally did get up enough nerve to tell Mom about Dorothy when we were sanding rocks together, and she listened quietly. Then, she stopped sanding and looked at me over her reading glasses.

"Are you telling me that you flew with this woman and that's how you got the cut on your forehead? Or was this just a dream you had?" Mom asked, brushing my hair out of my eyes.

I shrugged back, afraid to say what I believed. "It was a dream I guess."

Mom looked relieved. "Grace, honey, when you were just a baby, I would whisper to you that I wanted you to be like Peter Pan. I wished that you would never grow up," Mom said, standing to fetch a coarser piece of sandpaper. When she sat back down, she looked into my face again. "But if you can find a way to nurture that imagination of yours, well then, that's just as good as being young forever. Always find an outlet for your creativity and foster its growth."

I guess she didn't believe me about my flight. And now, without the distraction of sculpture or homework, my mind is swirling about Dorothy and that night all over again. Riding down Sunny's wide street that dead ends into a field of dandelions, memories of the mysterious flight circle through my mind. It's time to talk to someone who will actually believe my story.

Chapter 11: Up For Adventure

Thankfully, Sunny is waiting for me on her porch, wearing her boyfriend's wrestling sweatshirt. She is the only one of my friends with a serious boyfriend, which seems so weird. Boys are pretty much a mystery to me, although I have a terrible crush on Dennis's best friend, and maybe Karla's brother. I find it difficult to form sentences when they're around.

"Hey!" Sunny greets me, waving her hand. Her real name is Sunshine, and if anyone asks her where her name came from, her reply is, "My parents were traveling hippies when I was born and they couldn't decide on 'Earth' or 'Sunshine' as my name. They were at Red Rocks, at a concert in the pouring rain when my mom went into labor."

I lay my bike in the grass and walk up to sit on the porch next to her. "Hey, I survived captivity."

Sunny laughs, but she's clearly distracted.

"What's up?" I ask, noticing that there aren't any cars in her driveway. Sunny's family leaves her alone all the time. I lose track of where they go, but it seems like they have such important things to do, and Sunny is left to entertain herself. It's quite the contrast to my mom's house.

"Are your parents home?" I ask.

"No, Rick got called into work and Mom's in Denver for the day." She waves to her neighbor who she's been staring at since I rode up. The guy is shirtless, pushing a red lawnmower over patches of grass in the lot next door. It's really not that warm outside, so his bare chest is a not-so-subtle ploy to impress my friend. The boy is at least Tom's, my older brother, age, and has long, black hair. He smiles and waves back at Sunny.

"Isn't he dreamy?" she asks me, beaming with a mouth full of braces. "He just moved in."

I widen my eyes and nod back, amazed at how bold Sunny can be sometimes.

"He was blasting Van Halen in his garage earlier," she says with a lilt in her voice.

"Oh, he is cute then." I smile at him too now. "Since your parents are gone, do you want to ride out to the airport with me?" I ask.

"I thought you couldn't go out there anymore," she says, tearing her eyes away from the longhaired boy.

"I don't know." I shrug. "I figure if it's okay to ride my bike to your house, then I can probably ride out there too." I'm trying to reason this out.

Sunny rolls her eyes at me, which I cannot stand. "But why do you even want to? I thought it drove you crazy being out there all summer."

"It did, but I can't stop thinking about what happened that night," I say, fishing a rock out of my shoe to toss into the grass. "I want to figure this out. I want to see if I can go flying with Dorothy!"

"The lady from your dream? How are you supposed to do that, fall asleep out there again?"

Sunny is one of my greatest friends, but I'm beginning to wonder if I picked the wrong person to talk to. She's so matter-of-fact that her reaction reminds me of my Dad's when I tried to tell him about my dream, totally uninterested. I watch her neighbor struggle to avoid staring at us while Sunny smiles coyly back at him. Now it's my turn to roll my eyes.

"Sunny," I protest, vying for her interest, "I don't think it was a dream."

She looks confused. "What are you talking about, Grace? You think it really happened?"

I have her full attention now. "Ok, well, I told you about Dorothy's jacket, right? About how I almost sat on it and then I noticed the patch?"

Sunny stares at me blankly. "I don't remember the jacket. Is Dorothy the lady that was flying the plane?"

"Yeah," I say, miffed at my friend's attention span. "Anyway, when I woke up that night in the airplane, this was sitting in my lap." I pull the patch out of the front pocket of my jeans and show it to Sunny.

She's not impressed. "So, what is it?"

"Look at the name! Dorothy Morrow. That was the pilot. That was the patch on her jacket!"

She raises her hand. "Wait...what? Tell me the whole story again."

So I do. I tell Sunny everything I can remember about that night at the airport. I describe the dream of flying with Dorothy as best as I can recall. I tell her about Karl's accident and the firefighters that came to the field, the cut on my head, everything. She listens to the entire story without saying a word until I mention my encounter with Henry.

"Freaky," Sunny says. "Why didn't you tell me about the patch before?" She shivers like she has the chills.

"I thought I did. Maybe we ran out of time."

We sit silently for a while and then she asks, "Were the firefighters cute?"

I laugh and stand up, stretching my legs as Sunny clutches the brown and red patch in her hand. I wait for her to laugh or say that she is kidding and she really thinks I'm nuts.

Thankfully, Sunny looks up at me and raises her eyebrows. "I want to fly with Dorothy too. Come on, let's go out there!"

Sunny and I snatch a couple of granola bars from her cupboard, stash them in her backpack, and climb on our bicycles, ready for the long ride to the airport. We ride pretty quickly, not even stopping to jump off the tree swing as we pass by it. We are on a mission and I feel a rush of adrenaline as I lead us to an old wooden bridge that crosses the canal.

I was so excited to begin our adventure that I didn't stop to think about my dad. I'm certain that he's working in his hangar today. If he sees me out there, sneaking around airplanes, things could get ugly all over again.

"I didn't think about my dad, Sunny!" I yell back to her and she looks puzzled. "He'll be pissed if he sees me out at the field sneaking around, so we have to be careful."

"Why would he care?" she yells back. "We'll just tell him we wanted to go for a ride!" Sunny smiles at me like it's no big deal.

"All right, well, I'll be able to see if his truck is parked outside his hangar after we get around these trees. If he's there, we have to be careful he doesn't see us."

I know the paths around here better than any neighborhood in town, which will make for a quick getaway if we're spotted by anyone inside the main hangar. It's strange to tiptoe around the airfield I grew up on, but after the commotion last month, I certainly don't want to draw any more attention to myself. Besides, being on a mission is much more exhilarating.

We round some tall weeds and I see Dad's red pickup truck parked outside, but the large door on his hangar is closed. Good, this might work.

We either have to cross through the front parking lot of the airport and ride across the wide ramp, dodging between parked airplanes, or sneak through a field to get to Betty. I decide on the field, since the airport looks pretty empty and Dad's hangar faces the ramp.

I can't even say why I think we'll find a sign of Dorothy in Beached Betty, but I don't know where else to start. The airplane Dorothy was flying seems awfully similar to the weathered twin-engine plane I use as shelter from thunderstorms.

Sunny and I lay our bikes in the weeds about twenty yards from Betty and kneel down to formulate a plan. We will have to move quickly if anyone sees us, since the getaway path isn't right next to the plane. I suppose as long as Henry the Hawk Eye isn't sitting outside, we shouldn't have any problems.

"Ok. I'll go first, since I know how to get the door open," I tell Sunny. "When I wave to you, make sure it's clear on your side, and then you run over."

"Ok. I'll keep watch. What should I do if I see someone coming?" she asks eagerly.

"Uh, I don't know...can you still whistle with your braces on?"

Sunny purses her lips and repeatedly blows as hard as she

can. "I guess not," she says, but I'm laughing too hard to stop her from trying again. Soon we are both laughing and tears are streaming down our cheeks. I pick up a couple sticks near the ramp and tell Sunny to hide in the weeds and bang them together if someone comes.

"Sounds good," she agrees. "Is that the airplane?" She points in the direction of Betty, but she is hidden behind a couple of new Pipers parked nearby.

"It's the big plane right next to the cottonwood tree," I say, pointing to the old silver plane with the sun glinting off its wings.

"Wow, it's so cool looking! You actually flew in that airplane? I want to see what it looks like inside."

"Ok, I'm going for it," I say as Sunny grabs my arm.

"So, you'll wave when the door is open?" she asks anxiously.

"Yeah, then you run over."

I look at all three hangar doors and the parking lot, search the sky and listen for any airplanes coming in to land, and then run over to Betty. As I get closer, I notice she looks different somehow. The bumps in her metal skin are really prominent today, perhaps because of the mid-afternoon sun. But they remind me of the hail Dorothy and I were showered with.

I duck below the wing, heading straight for the tail wheel and the wrench to open the door. It's gone. I always leave it in the grass next to the wheel, but it's not here. I get on my hands and knees and stir through the underbrush, but there's no sign of it anywhere. Great. This could change things. I look back at Sunny and she is crouched behind weeds, ready to run over to me. I shake my head and make a cutthroat sign, hoping she can see.

It's getting frustrating trying to push, and then pull, on the door, working it open with my hands. I cross behind the airplane, hunting for the wrench, when I hear a knocking sound coming from Sunny's direction.

"Are you looking for this, Grace?"

I jump about three feet in the air and turn and see my dad

holding the very wrench I'm searching for. He doesn't look happy.

"Hey Dad. I was just...I wanted to show Sunny something," I stammer.

"Really, Grace? Are you sure you and your friend weren't trying to sneak around the airport to break into this plane right under my nose? Didn't your Mom tell you she didn't want you out here?" He is standing over me now and I'm wondering what has happened to Sunny.

"Well, she didn't really…" I try to reply, but he cuts me off.

"Go get your bikes and I'll put them in the back of the truck, Grace. I have to run into town, so I'll take you back to your mom's." Dad turns his back, not even giving me a chance to argue.

I wave to my friend and she comes out of the underbrush, looking as disappointed as I feel. We don't say much to each other as Dad loads our bikes into the back of his truck, but I feel Sunny tug on the back of my shirt. I look back at her and she nods her head toward something in the distance and whispers, "Is that the scary man?"

I turn my head to spot Henry, leaning against his closed hangar door with his arms crossed against his chest. There's no denying that he is staring right at us.

"Dad, how did you know we were out here?" I ask, suspicious of the old man.

"It's a small airport, Grace. Word passes pretty quickly," he replies, waving to Henry.

I have my answer. Why does it seem like Henry's out to get me? I look at Sunny as we climb into the cab. "He's right out of a horror film, isn't he?"

She laughs.

Chapter 12: Forbidden

Dad drives Sunny and me almost the entire way back into town without saying a word. He smokes cigarette after cigarette while I sit and stare out my window, wondering what my punishment will be. I realize this must be uncomfortable for my poor friend because she's wedged between Dad and me. Thankfully, she breaks the silence by asking him questions about his airplane. He actually lightens up a fair bit, and by the time we get to Sunny's house, Dad is somewhat cheerful. I'm impressed at her knowledge and finesse.

I had forgotten about the time Sunny went flying with Dad and me a couple summers ago. He let her sit in the front seat, where I usually get to sit, because it offers the best view. At first, she was petrified. But by the time we had landed and were taxiing back to Dad's hangar, Sunny was chirping about how much fun flying is. She said she wanted to take lessons as soon as she was old enough. It was all she talked about for an entire week at school. Then boys came along.

Since Dad's mood has lightened over the past fifteen minutes, I figure I may still be able to go to Karla's house for a sleepover tonight. Sunny and I were both invited and I've been looking forward to popcorn, junk food, and scary movies all week. Dad parks in front of Sunny's house and we quickly make plans to meet up as he unloads her bicycle from the truck.

Unfortunately, without Sunny's conversation skills, the ride to Mom's house is uncomfortably silent. The only relief from the silence is the announcer's voice on the radio, highlighting scores from some football game. Dad doesn't say a word. It's tough to tell if he's angry or lost in thought, but now is not the time to push my luck, so I unlatch my door and start to climb out of the truck as soon as we are parked. Dad grabs my arm. "Wait a minute, Grace."

I turn around, anticipating a reprimand, but Dad looks

flustered, like he's calculating his next words.

"There's something I need to talk to you about. We have to discuss what happened that night you missed the picnic," he says, finally.

My heart sinks. "What do you mean, Dad?" I notice he hasn't shaved for a couple days at least and his eyes are red. He looks tired.

"You know, Grace, that night, when you were sleeping. Did you…see anyone lurking around the airport, or did you notice anything strange going on around the ramp?" he asks.

"I guess. I mean, the whole night was strange, Dad."

He lets go of my arm and relaxes into the seat cushion. "Your mother is right, Grace. It's unsafe. I've had strange things happen to me out there and I just don't think you should be climbing around in those old airplanes."

I just stare back at him as my right leg dangles from the seat. "Are you alright, Dad? What strange things are you talking about?"

He turns off the ignition and his voice becomes grave. "I've taken it for granted that your brothers haven't been around all summer. And I have let you run around the airport, pretty much unsupervised for three months," Dad says, holding up his hand like he always does when I try to interrupt. "Now, I will not keep asking you how you got the cut on your forehead."

Good thing, because I cannot come up with any more excuses. Though I have no proof, I'm pretty sure it's from the yoke with the shiny B on it.

"And I'm not even going to tell you what your mother suggests happened that night." He raises his eyebrows at me. He's right. I don't want to know.

"Anyway, with this new company trying to buy the field and Ted breathing down my neck, I'm afraid people are scouting out the land when they shouldn't be. I have a bad feeling and I've seen some odd folks out there lately, Grace. It isn't safe for a young lady to be running around by herself." Dad feigns a smile as if to soften the blow. "Even a tough young lady, got it?"

Where is this coming from? "Dad, I've pretty much grown up out there with you. It's fine. It's like my second home," I say with a laugh, hoping to lighten him up. But he isn't listening.

"I don't care. I don't want you going in that old Beech anymore, nor any of the other airplanes on the ramp," Dad says, fixing his gaze outside the windshield.

"Dad, you don't have to worry about me getting hurt. I mean there's something I really need to..."

"Grace," he interrupts me and there is anger behind his eyes. "Even though it's a small airport and everyone knows each other, those fences aren't big enough to keep strangers out. Besides, there are screws and bits of metal sticking out everywhere inside that old airplane...I almost sliced my own forehead open trying to get you out of there."

"Is that really why you're worried, Dad, because of some screws and parts lying around?" I ask, indignant now. "Dad, I'm careful. Besides, I like hanging out in that old plane. It's the only place I can go where no one bothers me. All of my drawing stuff, even my journal, is inside it."

"I know, G," Dad says, watching Mom's station wagon pass by as she turns to park in her driveway. "But we're going to have to get your stuff out of the plane."

This is ridiculous. "Are you grounding me from the airplane too?" I ask, unable to hide my frustration. Now I'll never learn about Dorothy or what happened that night!

"Come on, G, let's get your bike. I've already had this discussion with your mother and I'm not interested in doing it again. I have to get going," Dad says, pushing his door open.

Mom takes a long time to get out of her car. I'm sure she must be wondering why Dad is dropping me off. I silently plead with him not to say anything about me being at the airport today.

"Dad, how much would it cost to just buy Betty?" I ask, hoping to distract him.

"Why, you going to get a job?" Dad laughs as he picks my bike out of the back of his pickup.

83

"You're too late, G. Henry has been tracking down the owners to see if they'll sell. Apparently he wants to add the Beech 18 to his fleet, so we need to empty it out."

"Henry? He wants to buy that old airplane? What the heck would he do with it?" I ask, confused.

Dad slams the truck gate shut and it feels like someone has slapped me in the face. I take my bike from his bumper and watch the truck until it turns a corner, disappearing from sight, and rumbling through the neighborhood.

Why does Henry want to buy Beached Betty?

Chapter 13: A Minor Setback

Since my father dropped me off at Mom's house and then left in such a hurry, I figured it was unnecessary to tell Mom about Sunny and I failing to break into Beached Betty. Such information is superfluous. She seemed satisfied when I explained that Dad had picked me up and given me a ride home and, thankfully, she didn't ask where he found me. I didn't tell.

So I filled up my backpack with all the necessary items for a sleepover and headed to Karla's house before the sun went down, and before Mom could change her mind about letting me go. The chill in the air was noticeable, but I still enjoyed the freedom of pedaling through town and watching kids play in the neighborhoods, enjoying their final moments of sunshine.

When I arrive at my friend's house, Sunny is already there and the two girls are outside, helping Karla's older brother, Jimmy, lift the family boat onto a trailer. Jimmy is her oldest brother, and Sunny and I refer to him as "Greek God." His light brown hair has streaks of blond, highlighted by the sun, and, even in the winter, his skin is somehow tanned. I've yet to see eyes as deep blue as his and they pierce through me whenever he looks in my direction. Anytime Jimmy actually speaks to me, I become a stuttering idiot. It's humiliating.

I watch as Jimmy connects the trailer to the hitch on the back of his jeep. His white t-shirt and green and blue swim shorts cling to his lean muscles and I'm certain the only reason Sunny volunteered to help is so that she could stare at such a fine specimen. I should have come earlier too.

I wave at Sunny and Karla as they steal a ride up the driveway in the back of the boat. Beyond them the water looks inviting, so I walk out to the dock to take a closer look.

Karla's backyard is almost the size of our high school football field. Bordered by tall pine trees, it backs up to the only lake in town and is the best place to spend a hot summer day. If

Karla isn't at camp, she is likely to be traveling with her family to some exotic place during the summer months. So it's a treat when her friends get invited to a slumber party. Even in the middle of winter, we can find plenty to do.

A sleepover mostly consists of popcorn, soda, and scary movies, and then the telling of ghost stories until the wee hours of the morning. But the last one ended with six of us girls knocking on the neighbor's door in our pajamas because we thought someone was in the house. It turned out to be another one of Karla's brothers, playing a trick, but we were thoroughly freaked out.

I plunk myself down on the very end of the dock, letting my feet hover over the water. Small waves lap against the wood supports as I gaze across to the other side of the lake. It is so peaceful out here where the towering pine trees narrow the sky and the water stretches out for at least a mile. It's a small lake, but grand homes and boat docks reach out into the water, cluttering much of its shoreline. Karla's backyard is usually a social center when the family is in town, but not today.

"AH!" Hands clasp my shoulders and for a second, I am sure I'm going into the water. I grab the hands and turn around to see Jimmy's blue eyes laughing back.

"So close," he says, smiling at me with Karla and Sunny giggling right behind him.

I smile back and notice Jimmy's perfectly straight teeth and his crooked smile. It steals all sound from my lips.

Thankfully, Sunny attempts to push Jimmy off the dock and his attention turns to her. We all tumble back to the yard to play Frisbee for a while.

The four of us eventually move inside, as the evening air grows cooler. Jimmy's girlfriend rings the doorbell and he leaves the three of us alone, sitting around the kitchen table.

As soon as he disappears, Sunny and I fill Karla in about the events earlier in the day. We make popcorn on the stove and I repeat the entire story of the night at the airport for Karla's benefit, while Sunny interrupts me to accentuate certain parts.

"Why would you wait until today to tell us this story?" Karla asks, dumbfounded.

"Actually, I told you both all about Dorothy during study hour on the first day of school, remember?"

Karla shakes her head.

"I even brought Dorothy's patch with me that day, but I didn't get to show it to you before Eric interrupted us."

"Well, you can't leave the patch out! It's the coolest part of the story!" Karla shouts.

Sunny laughs, stuffing a handful of popcorn in her mouth. "Yeah, it's not really a minor detail, Grace."

Karla sits quietly, processing something. Then she leans forward toward Sunny and me with her eyes wide and whispers, "Let's go out there tonight."

"What?" I jump back and almost knock a picture frame off the wall behind me. "To the airport?"

Karla smiles at my clumsiness.

"Absolutely not, are you kidding? If I get caught out there, my parents won't let me see the light of day for the rest of the year...I'll be locked in the basement." I look at Sunny for support. "Besides, Henry is probably waiting for us to try to break into that airplane again."

Sunny nods and looks at Karla. "Yeah, he is one creepy old dude."

But Karla is too excited to hear any of this. "No one will even see us. I've got flashlights we can duct tape to our bikes and then use them to check out the airplane when we get there."

"No way," I argue. "The airport is like, ten miles away, and it's probably freezing outside by now!"

"SHHH." Karla points to the open doorway. "It's not that cold. Besides, Jimmy is going to his girlfriend's house pretty soon. If we wait until he leaves, my parents won't be home until late and they'll just think we're asleep if the door is closed."

"And then what?" I ask. "What about the morning, when we aren't in bed?"

Judi Stephenson

"I'm not saying we spend the night out there, are you nuts?" Karla says in a loud whisper. "Let's just go and see if we can make the airplane fly again. I want to check it out. I want to meet Dorothy! We can sneak back in through my window. And, on the way, let's stop by Lynn's house and see if she and Marie want to come!"

I sigh when I see the look on Sunny's face. She knows just as well as I do that it's impossible to win an argument against Karla. I guess we're going to try this search for Dorothy again. The thought sends a chill down my spine.

The three of us girls, dressed in black, flashlights taped to our bicycles, is a hilarious sight. How likely is it we will ride across town, cross railroad tracks, ramble over dirt roads and potholes, and break into an airplane with no one spotting us? Before I can give it another thought, Sunny has adjusted the backpack carrying our supplies and we are beginning our journey.

We stop at Lynn's house and toss rocks against her window but she doesn't answer. It's probably a good thing because the three of us will be loud enough clamoring around at the airport.

It's after midnight when we reach the dark airfield. Karla fell off her bike twice, but stayed in good spirits. My flashlight went dead. I stopped to shake up the batteries, but it still wouldn't work, so I had to ride close behind Sunny.

But we made it. Now I have to find Betty on the dark ramp. There are only two lights illuminating the main hangar tonight. One is lighting up the large sliding door and the other shines on the side door. Dad has turned off the light above his sign, and Henry's single bulb is flickering above the side entrance to his own hangar. Though the lights on the main hangar are intense, they only illuminate a circle of pavement beneath them. And clouds obscure the moon, so it's going to be difficult to see even twenty feet in front of us without flashlights. I'm leery of being spotted, even if it is late.

"Okay," I say, taking a deep breath. "Let's get the flashlights off the bikes and leave them at the edge of the

88

parking lot. The airplane isn't far from here."

"What if we need to make a fast getaway?" Karla has already removed her flashlight and holds it under her chin. "I mean, what if someone's waiting for us with a pitchfork..."

Sunny slaps Karla on the arm. "Stop it! I'm already freaked out!"

I laugh. "Come on, it's cold! We have to keep moving."

I lead us to Betty pretty quickly as Sunny hands me the wrench we stashed inside her backpack. It takes some time to get the door open, and the familiar, musty smell wafts out toward us.

"Why would you ever want to come out here and fall asleep in this old airplane, Grace? It's like a horror movie out here." Sunny looks at me, shuddering.

"It's cool inside though. Come on, you just have to check it out." I climb in first and hold the door open for them to follow.

As I move toward the cockpit, my dream floods back. I don't see the pictures posted in the back of the airplane or the cushions stacked against the beanbag on the dirty, worn-out carpet. Instead, I envision the neatly upholstered interior with soft, cushioned seats. As I walk forward, I remember Dorothy's profile and the instruments that were alive, their needles dancing in the turbulence.

"Wow, how long has this plane been sitting here?" Karla asks, standing behind me.

"I don't know. Ever since I can remember, though." I sit in the left seat and Karla slides into the right side. Sunny stands right behind us, shining her flashlight on the instrument panel.

"Everything looks so old. There's no way this thing can still fly, right?" Sunny pushes one of the levers forward and I look down at the cluster of them. Why didn't I notice how many levers this airplane had before?

"Well, it has to be able to fly 'cause she flew with Dorothy, remember?" Karla prods Sunny.

"I can't believe you guys came out here with me. It's weird to be sitting here after all that happened. It's like I'm seeing it all over again."

"I want to talk to Dorothy," Karla says, her eyes darting between Sunny and me. "Don't you guys? I mean, isn't that why we came all the way out here?" She shines her flashlight outside the window. "Maybe we should have brought our sleeping bags."

"No way!" Sunny shouts. "I am definitely not camping out here. Some psycho is probably sitting behind a tree, watching us right now!"

"Shh, wait!" I grab for Karla's flashlight and tilt it toward the ground. "Turn your light off!" I whisper despite the rush of adrenaline surging through my veins.

Sunny crouches down onto her knees. "What? Is somebody out there?"

"I could swear I just saw someone walking around in front of that hangar. Do you guys see anyone over there?" I ask, pointing to Henry's old, metal building, which houses who knows what.

With our flashlights extinguished, it takes my eyes several seconds to adjust to the darkness again.

"You mean the building with the spooky flickering bulb over there?" Sunny asks.

"Yeah, it looks like someone is inside the hangar," I say, pointing again.

"I see them too! They just walked past the window!" Karla pauses. "Is it the creepy man's place?"

Sunny looks back at me and nods. "It is, right? Why would he be out here at this time of night? He's older than my grandpa and *he* goes to bed way before the sun goes down. What do you think he's doing all by himself in there?"

Karla crouches down on the floorboards. "Who says he's by himself? Maybe he has dead bodies in there!"

"Shut UP, Karla!" Sunny protests. "I don't know why I let you guys drag me out to this scary place! If I weren't so freaked out, I'd ride home and leave you both out here!"

"Shh, I'm sure Henry is just out here working on his old airplane or something." I try to calm Sunny down, but the idea of getting out of here while we're ahead is pretty appealing. I turn to Karla. "You know, maybe she's right. I don't like being out here while Henry is messing around in his hangar. Who knows what he's doing in there."

I can feel Karla's brown eyes digging into me.

"Karla, we should get out of here. If there are dead bodies in that place…" Sunny's sentence trails off and we all stare at the old man's hangar.

"Then we should find out about them and call the police, don't you think?" Karla asks. She jumps up, bumping her head on the ceiling. "Don't you guys get it? We could be saving someone's life right now!" Karla grabs my arm. "Come on! Don't you realize what we have to do?"

Sunny and I exchange glances. "No," she replies.

"We have to go and spy on the creepy man!" Karla exclaims.

"No, Karla…no way," I say, expecting Sunny to agree with me, but she is watching the shadows moving across the window looking into Henry's hangar.

The small, framed glass next to his side door is usually dark and difficult to see into. I have always thought it was boarded from the inside, but tonight it is dancing with movement. The shadows make it look as though there are several people muddling about.

"I'll do it," Sunny exclaims and I stare back at her, shocked. She defends herself to me. "Come on, Grace, didn't you say you wonder why he's out here so much? Maybe we can figure out what he's up to. Maybe we actually would be saving somebody's life right now." Both girls are staring at me.

I think about riding home alone with no flashlight, leaving my friends here to get caught spying on Henry, knowing I wouldn't make it far in the darkness. It probably is the perfect opportunity to see what the old guy could be up to. "Fine. But I'm out of here so fast if he hears us."

"Without a flashlight?" Karla asks, grinning at me.

We close up the airplane as quietly as possible and make our way through the darkness.

I'm afraid Henry will catch us looking in the small window, as the flickering bulb is hanging right next to it. I motion for us to walk around to the opposite side of his hangar and spot a window I had never noticed before. Probably because it's on the side of the building facing an open pasture and the broken-down airplanes parked outside.

As we get closer, it becomes obvious that the window is too high for us to possibly see through. Karla must have noticed this as well. She whispers, "We can take turns standing on each others' backs to get a look in there."

We decide Karla should be first. Sunny and I get on our hands and knees in the dirt and grass next to the old airplanes as Karla climbs onto our backs. She raises herself onto her toes and they jab into my shoulder.

"Hurry up, Karla. Your toes are digging holes in my back," I whisper.

Her foot shifts and she jumps onto the ground. "It's really hard to see anything through that dirty window, but it looks like a garage with a lot of junk in it. There is a weird light coming from another room, though. I was trying to see the old man, but I couldn't see anyone."

"Here, let me try," I say as Sunny grudgingly gets onto her hands and knees again.

"Make it quick," Sunny groans, "my back cannot take much more."

I press myself against the building and the coldness of the metal reaches through my sweatshirt. I tolerate it as I peer through the window, hoping to take in as much as I can. I see the tail of an airplane, shelves of tools against the back wall, and lots of photographs and framed certificates, impossible to read from this distance. It looks like piles of stuff are all over the floor. Karla is right, there is a changing light coming from an open doorway. Maybe it's a television. As I search for a sign of Henry, my eyes are drawn to some black and white photos on a partition.

"Ugh!" Sunny collapses beneath my weight and I drop sideways into the tall weeds. Karla starts laughing so hard that soon all three of us are giggling in the shadows.

"Shh, you guys!" I say, catching my breath. I cannot help laughing at how ridiculous this whole adventure has turned out to be.

"I'm sorry! My back couldn't take it anymore," Sunny says, stifling laughter.

The creaking sound of a door opening around the corner of the hangar makes us all sit straight up to listen.

"Who's there?" It's a man's voice. It has to be Henry. "Who's out there?" he shouts again.

It takes my brain about thirty seconds to catch up to my feet, running as fast as I can to get my bicycle. I hear Sunny and Karla behind me, giggling and tripping over one another.

I ride about ten feet into the darkness and crash into a pothole. Karla turns on her flashlight and is strapping it to her bicycle like she has done it a thousand times before. I follow her guidance and after an interminable amount of time, we are peddling our way off the dirt road and onto paved, familiar streets with lights to brighten our paths. Karla turns around, looks at us, and just starts cracking up.

"Ahhh, that was crazy!" She is yelling and at this point, I couldn't care less about the noise. I'm just grateful we made it out without Henry catching us.

My body is numb from the cold as we turn onto Karla's street. The entire row of homes backs up to the lake and I notice a mist rolling off the water behind her house. By the time we stash our bikes on the side of Karla's garage, a thin layer of fog is hanging above the grass around her house. We sneak inside and Karla brings hot chocolate and pop tarts into her bedroom as we slowly defrost, spending the next hour or so giggling and recounting the night's events.

Chapter 14: October Skies

In the following weeks, I find it extremely difficult to concentrate in school. Every day, especially in English class, I am mesmerized by the colorful leaves outside the window, which then distract my mind onto a variety of paths.

Mostly, I think about flying. My mind travels through memories of soaring above the earth with my father and slicing through clouds with Dorothy. I wonder if my daydreaming is the reason Ms. Drags, my history teacher, has begun to close the blinds in the classroom. I like reading about certain events or cultures and how they've evolved over time, but my teacher makes it duller than studying patterns in cement. And without sunlight, the fluorescent bulbs are invasive, turning the room into a prison cell, which doesn't help me focus; it just makes me want to run out of class and keep running.

Today I'm so anxious to get out of the building that I don't stick around to talk to friends after the final bell rings. I unlock my bike from the metal rack and begin the ride to Mom's house.

The air is cool and my fingers turn red as the wind whips around them, so I release the handles and hide my hands inside the sleeve of my sweatshirt.

As I balance my weight and coast over the asphalt, I think of the night with Karla and Sunny and how the fog had taken over the neighborhood as we were putting our bikes away. And when I fell asleep inside Beached Betty on the evening I flew with Dorothy, there had been a thunderstorm and a mist clouded the air right before I must have been knocked out. The same night, Karl said he had landed in fog behind another plane, while Dorothy and I had to search for the airport through a layer of white. It was even lingering when Dad drove me home that night.

Is the secret in the fog? Maybe when the land is obscured, maybe that is when Beached Betty flies again. Hasn't it always seemed like Betty has a personality of her own? It would sound ridiculous to say it out loud, but I wonder if I should go back out to the airport on a foggy night. Perhaps that's the secret. I can certainly try. Maybe I could even see Dorothy again and talk to her, find out where she came from and how she learned to fly that airplane. And what was in Casper? Didn't she say she had to deliver the plane to a General?

I stash my bike next to mom's garage and head inside for some yogurt as my thoughts morph into a plan. First, I need to figure out when the fog will come, since it really doesn't happen too often.

At dinner, Mom asks several questions about school and I give the briefest answers possible. Truthfully, my grades are lower than they've ever been, but I'm struggling to get motivated to write an essay about a book that I lost interest in after page two or to do exercises in dull textbooks. I want to read about Dorothy and where she learned to fly. I want to read about adventures in the air. I want to learn about where fog comes from.

After drying the dinner plates and stacking them in Mom's cupboard, I excuse myself to go and dig through my closet for an aviation book Dad gave me a few months ago. I remember that it had a section on meteorology.

By nine thirty, I have learned that fog forms when the temperature and dew point are close together. I'm not sure what that means, but the book lists a few conditions, which may apply to the airport. Fog forms on a humid night when the wind is light and the ground is cool. Or it might occur when the warm air settles above the colder water of a lake and then rolls down the hill to the airfield. The most likely event in the summer would be after a rainstorm, as fog can develop from precipitation.

Mom taking the book from my hands and sitting on the edge of my bed awakens me. She flips though a few pages and knits her eyebrows.

"Hey, Mom, what time is it?" I ask, sitting up against my headboard.

"It's too late for you to be reading." Mom tilts her head and looks at me. "Did your father give you this?" she asks, closing the book to check out the cover.

"Yeah, a while ago. I was just looking something up."

"For school?" she asks, smirking.

I shake my head. "No. I was reading about fog."

Mom sets the book on the shelf above my desk, next to the thesaurus I hardly use. "Fog? In an aviation book?"

"Aviation Meteorology, Mom," I correct her.

"Excuse me." She turns to face me with her hands on her hips. "First of all, you should be doing homework before you look at any of this flying gibberish. And second, I'm betting fog and flying don't go well together, and what more would you possibly need to know?" She smiles and kisses me on the forehead and shuts off the light by my bed. "Sleep tight, Grace."

"Good night, Mom," I say, staring at the glow of the hall light on the ceiling. I wonder if this is a bad idea, going to the airport alone. Maybe Dad is right. Maybe it is dangerous out there. I'm anxious to tell Karla and Sunny about it tomorrow but also nervous they might think I've gone over the edge. Or, maybe they'd be willing to come with me?

My friends both laugh at me when I tell them what I've been planning. Karla shows interest in accompanying me to the airport at first, but she and Sunny both become skeptical when I mention that it would have to be at night...in the fog. I guess the idea of riding to the airport with sleeping bags in tow and trying to spend the night in a dirty old airplane around Halloween is just plain scary. Also, it isn't rare to have snow at the end of October, so how can I blame them?

It looks like I'm going on this mission alone. I console myself with the fact that Dennis used to camp out in the woods several nights by himself to earn merit badges when he was my age. He even had to dig out a snow cave and spend more than one night huddling inside it. If he could manage to survive that, then surely I can spend a night in old Betty.

Chapter 15: Perseverance

I made it through the rest of the school week, thanks to relief from my algebra teacher. Mr. C is probably the coolest adult I know and I'm lucky he teaches the one subject that isn't very interesting. Just when the formulas are forcing half the class to draw mindlessly in their notebooks, he breaks up the monotony by throwing erasers at people and spitting his gum across the room. It certainly gets my attention and usually a good laugh from the rest of the kids. He isn't just a math teacher; he's sort of a counselor for all of us.

I had been looking forward to the weekend, planning to have a sleepover at Dad's house. Karla and I were going to put together our Halloween costumes using his old mechanic uniforms and flight stuff. And Dad usually buys us snacks and lets us stay up late watching movies. But at the last minute, he had to drive Cindy to Cheyenne to visit her brother in the hospital. No sleepover.

Instead, I'm spending a Saturday night watching Mom flutter between her bathroom and bedroom, getting ready for her first date since she divorced my father. It's strange to think Mom would be nervous to have dinner with a man after having three kids with my Dad. I thought she had seen it all, but she's acting like I do whenever I see Karla's brother.

Mom pops out of her bedroom wearing the sixth sweater I've seen her try on with a long plaid skirt. "Are you sure you'll be okay here tonight?" She asks me for the third time.

"Mom! I'm fourteen and I'm the only one of my friends who is not trusted to be left alone. Besides, most of my friends are babysitters."

She steps into the bathroom and fastens the back of her earring, "I don't care about the rest of your friends. They aren't *my* kids."

We argue as I stand in front of the television, switching the knob to find a good show to distract my thoughts. The knob comes off in my hand and I have to fiddle with it to get it to work again. Where is Dukes of Hazzard? Shouldn't Charlie's Angels be starting soon? The clearest channel is showing the local news, so I watch for a few minutes, hoping that Charlie's Angels will be next. The meteorologist is circling an area north of Denver and talking about fog in the forecast for tonight. Fog? She's pointing right at our town! Hmm, Mom won't be home most of the night. I don't have a babysitter...

"MOM!" I yell, reminding myself not to sound excited or she'll suspect something's up.

She leans her head out of the bathroom, "Grace, I'm right here. You don't have to shout."

"Sorry. Would it make you feel better if I stay at Sunny's house tonight?"

"I thought she was visiting her cousin in Denver. Isn't that what you told me, Grace?" She narrows her eyes and looks at me, suspecting something.

Now I have to choose my words carefully. "No, I guess she came back early with her sister, Daisy."

"But her parents aren't home?"

"No, but her sister will be. They came back early to catch a matinee. I'm sure they're home by now," I stammer.

This is partially true. Sunny did come home early, but her sister is probably halfway to Denver by now to visit her boyfriend.

Mom is watching my every move. "Grace, it's nearly six o'clock. Why didn't you ask me about this earlier?"

The doorbell rings and I'm saved from answering her question. Mom's date, Robert, is a friend of her best friend's husband. She lets out a nervous sigh and turns off the bathroom light, brushing her fingers across her forehead.

"You look great, Mom," I tell her as she flashes an anxious smile and opens the front door. Poor Robert looks terrified as he waves awkwardly at me, holding a small vase of flowers.

After the strained introductions, Mom tells Robert she'll be outside in a moment and his shoulders immediately sink as he steps onto the porch again. She zips her purse, takes a final look into the mirror, and then points her finger in my direction. "Grace, you can spend the night at Sunny's house, but that is exactly what you're doing. I don't want you going out with her sister, or sneaking out for any reason, got it?" She is looking at me now. "Will Daisy come and pick you up?"

"Thanks, Mom." I jump up from the couch, excited to get packing. "I think I'll just ride my bike."

"You will not ride your bike in the dark, young lady, and it will be dark in half an hour."

"Mom, it will take me less than ten minutes to get to her house."

She walks over and tousles my hair. "Then you have exactly five minutes to get your things together and get moving, or else you will be staying home. And I want you back by eleven tomorrow, understand?" she asks, closing the door behind her after I nod in submission.

I feel guilty all of a sudden. But what do I do? This is the perfect opportunity for an adventure! Soon the snow will fall and the temperatures will be way too cold for my thin sleeping bag to handle. Besides, if it doesn't work, I can put this mystery to rest and focus on school again. I haven't had any interest in classes since they began this semester.

Robert's car pulls away, and I spend the next few moments listing multiple reasons why I shouldn't go to the airport while racing around the house, gathering supplies: sleeping bag, long underwear, water, granola bars, journal (in case I want to take notes), and stick matches (in case I get stranded and need to light a fire). I find a second flashlight in the garage and toss it in my backpack, along with pliers to open the door to the airplane.

The sun has already fallen behind the mountains, but I may just have enough light to ride my bike to the airport. I have to leave soon. I almost forgot to call Sunny and let her know the plan. Thankfully, she answers.

"Why are you going out there tonight? You'll freeze!" she says through the phone. "They say it may even snow."

"No, the meteorologist just said there'd be fog. Besides, I

have to go out there, Sunny. It's my last chance. So, if my mom calls, tell her I'm sleeping or something."

"You are nuts, totally and absolutely nuts," she says, sighing in my ear. "Whatever. Don't you think you should wait until your brothers or someone can go with you?"

I don't know how to reply. Not because I disagree with her, but I'm baffled that Sunny is giving me responsible advice. "There's a phone in Dad's hangar if I get into trouble. I'll call you in the morning."

"Just come over as soon as you wake up. I want to hear what happens."

"Ok, thanks a lot, Sunny. I'll see you tomorrow." I hang up the receiver and the feeling of foreboding returns.

The ride out to the airport from Mom's house is much quicker than from Karla's house. It helps that I can take a shortcut. But the sunlight disappears sooner than I had anticipated, making it tough to see the bumps in the rough road. And the temperature has dropped significantly, which inspires me to pedal hard to stay warm.

I round the dirt path to see that Dad's parking spot in front of his hangar is empty. Henry's building looks vacant too. It's hard to tell though, as he always seems to be lurking in the shadows somewhere. Regardless, I move furtively, hiding my bike in the weeds behind the cottonwood tree and then making my way to Betty. The door opens easily with the help of Mom's pliers and I throw my backpack and sleeping sack inside and climb in.

"All right, Betty, it is you and me," I say, setting up camp. I'm proud of myself for bringing a bungee cord to hook to the door, in case someone tries to pry it open from the outside. It should be enough of a struggle that it wakes me up. I plan to keep Mom's long, metal flashlight in my sleeping bag to double as a weapon.

Four hours and a granola bar later, I am still wide-awake. I tried singing to myself, writing in my journal, and reading by the light of my smaller flashlight. Nothing has worked and now I have to go to the bathroom.

It takes a few minutes to remove the bungee contraption and survive the mission of going outside. If I wasn't so leery of being out here alone, I might be able to enjoy a peaceful night at the airfield.

Looking over at Henry's hangar, I notice the light above his door is putting off a steady, yellow glow. Thankfully, his side window is dark. Henry wouldn't have driven out to the airfield this late at night, would he? I didn't notice his outside light on earlier, but that's probably because it wasn't flickering like it was the last time I was out here.

There is a haze forming over the tall, brown grass. What few lights are out at the field are casting an eerie glow into the air. I guess the woman on the news was right. The fog must be coming in.

I climb into the airplane and tuck myself back into the insulated nylon bag to try again.

Chapter 16: The New Kid

I wake up sweating. The air is heavy and I try to push my sleeping bag off, but it isn't there. I look down at my body and the bright light all around me arrests my vision. I have to squint, giving my eyes time to adjust to the change.

It feels like I'm riding in the back of Dad's pickup truck. The air is hot and dry as the tires jostle over a rough road.

And then I remember my mission. I remember trying to fall asleep in the back of...Betty.

Did it work? I sit up and look at my surroundings. I'm in the back of an airplane, that's for certain, but I don't think it's flying. There are no pictures posted on the walls and the air is hot and muggy. My head feels like I've been on a roller coaster. I'm dizzy and disoriented, yet the feeling is oddly familiar.

The cabin of the plane is very basic. There are metal rails in the floor where seats should be and everything is covered in dust, even the windows. I can still see outside through the grime.

It's a challenge to decipher anything beyond all the dirt kicked up from the propellers. But it looks as though we're taxiing through the desert.

I crawl forward on my stomach to investigate the cockpit. There are two people up there. A man wearing a khaki shirt is sitting on the right side, but I can only see the sleeve of the person on the left. The man is gesturing and pointing at something.

I pull my knees up on the dirty floor beneath me and sit on my heels to get a better view. The curled, reddish hair looks familiar. The woman turns to look at her co-pilot and I immediately recognize Dorothy's profile.

"Dorothy!" The name comes out of my mouth before I can stop myself, but the pilots don't hear me. It's extremely loud and they're too busy watching the world outside the airplane and talking to one another. Both of them are wearing those funny headphones and the man appears to be speaking into the microphone. Dorothy nods her head in understanding. I get up a little closer, careful to not be seen.

The man points toward an airplane turning in front of us and says something I cannot discern. I watch as the airplane ahead to our left joins the line in front of us. There appears to be a line of planes stringing out ahead, but it's not possible to tell how many.

"So, Moore wasn't able to fly today? Is he not feeling well?" Dorothy shouts over the engines, ignoring the microphone.

The man shrugs his shoulders, staring straight ahead as Dorothy maneuvers the airplane down a stretch of pavement in the middle of a wide dirt path. An airplane takes off opposite our direction and I watch it slowly become airborne. It's a shiny silver bird with a large round nose housing a single propeller. Not long after it climbs above the pavement, another one follows. It looks like the very same model. It has a completely glass top, enclosing two pilots sitting tandem to one another. And it's loud. Even over our rumbling engines, I can almost feel its mighty takeoff.

Dorothy and her companion stop talking to one another as she taxies out to where the pavement ends, whirls the plane around to the right, and parks. The airplane ahead of us begins its takeoff roll. I cannot see any clear markings of designated runways or taxiways, but it's hard to see much with the nose of the airplane in the way. If nothing's marked, all the planes seem to know where they're going, like it's routine for them.

While we're parked, Dorothy moves several levers backward and forward. I see her glance at a piece of paper and then tuck it next to the window. She then slides the throttles forward and the power of the engines knocks me onto the floor. I have to hold tight to the metal rails to avoid tumbling to the rear of the plane as the air explodes around us and we accelerate down the runway, and then lift off the ground, into the clear blue sky.

We appear to be following the airplane ahead of us.

Dorothy repositions levers, looks over her shoulder, and turns the airplane to the left. I sit back on my heels to look out the windows at the cloudless sky above us. It may be hot and dusty on the ground, but up here it's a gorgeous day.

We turn above the large field we departed from, and I can see that there are buildings bordering it now. They are long and flat. From the air they look like houses from a monopoly game all lined up. As we turn again, I spot several airplanes lined up on the ground beneath us. I count nearly thirty of them, staggered into rows, and there's still a line of airplanes taxiing out to the takeoff position. I've never seen so many before.

Dorothy is flying a rectangular pattern above the runway, just like Dad taught me to do. On days that Dad wants me to work on takeoffs and landings, we will simply fly in the rectangular pattern over and over again. But instead of making a third left turn, Dorothy continues to climb straight ahead. The nose is pointed into the blue and the man speaks into the microphone again. Dorothy nods.

What a perfect day to fly. The air is smooth as silk and there are no clouds to be seen. The desert airfield we departed from soon fades into a small piece of the patchwork below. The arid land seems to go on forever. I jump to the other side of the plane to look at some low hills, sparsely decorated with trees as they lower to meet the far spanning plains. There is an unusual beauty about the landscape. I haven't seen anything like it.

My face is pressed to the window as the airplane banks sharply to the right. I lose my balance and fall to the other side of the plane, grappling for the metal rails to hold onto. Then another bank in the opposite direction pushes me flat on the rail, tearing a hole in my shirt and knocking my elbow against the hard floor.

I search for something stable and notice a small bucket seat propped against the partial wall separating the cabin from the cockpit. The pilots would have to lean out of their seats to see me sitting there, so I lunge for it. And just as I am figuring out the seat belt contraption, the rumbling sound of the

engines drops to a low purr. I crane my neck to look into the cockpit and see Dorothy calmly holding the throttles all the way back. And she's pulling on the yoke! Bad idea!

"Dorothy, stop!" I yell, but she doesn't hear me. She just keeps raising the nose of the plane up and the silence is more deafening than the engines were at full power.

"Dorothy, no!" It's too late. The nose of the airplane suddenly drops and shifts slightly to the left. We are falling out of the sky! A few seconds of this and Dorothy moves the throttles again and slowly raises the nose back to the horizon. The blaring sound of the engines returns and I let out a sigh of relief.

Curiosity takes over and I tear off the seat belt. I crouch behind the wall and get as close as possible to the cockpit without being seen. The man is talking through the microphone and I watch his lips move as I strain to hear his words over the drone of the engines. "And keep the nose straight this time until you want it to spin..." The man is making hand gestures, imitating an airplane climbing and then diving to the right.

Spin? Is he crazy? In this airplane? I thought only my dad's friend Neal could do those in his spunky little red airplane. Not a heavy bulldozer like this!

Dorothy pulls the throttles back again and my heart drops down to my knees. I jump back to the seat and fasten the belt again just in time. It's a ride.

We rise and fall, twisting and diving like a gymnast through the air. Every time we level out and I regain my bearings, the airplane starts a new routine of climbing and turning, stalling and diving. I wish I could see what Dorothy is doing, but whenever I lean out of my seat to have a look, I'm forced back down by gravity.

Panic rises into my throat as one of the engines is silenced. Sure enough, I look outside and the propeller on the left side is stopped completely and turned a strange angle into the wind stream. Immediately, I unclasp the seat belt to tell the pilot what I see, but as I'm about to spring into the cockpit, I hear the sound of it sputtering back to life! For the third or perhaps tenth time today, I'm immensely grateful for the sound of the engines as they hum together, running strong.

We finally begin our descent back to the earth and I peer through the windows to see the familiar field in the center of the dirt below us. My stomach is still caught in my throat, my scalp tingling, and possibly all the adrenaline stored in corners of my body is racing through my bloodstream, but I'm smiling. I sure wasn't prepared for that ride.

Dorothy lands firmly back on the runway and taxis behind another airplane to an open spot at the end of the row. She shuts down the engines and my ears ring from the noise. What now? We're parking and that's it? I'm thinking of how I can go up with them and do it all again, forgetting I still have to find a way to get home.

As Dorothy and the man converse, I quietly disconnect my seat belt and try to open the small door in the back of the airplane. Then I stop myself. Should I get out? What if this airplane my only ride home? I could just walk around and take a look at the place, right? I can always come back to the plane. Will I recognize it among all these others?

I hear the sound of a seatbelt disconnecting in the cockpit and the man instructing Dorothy to look the plane over, so I move fast. I push against the mysterious door but it won't budge. I test the main door. It pops out and I jump from the plane, just as Dorothy is climbing out of her seat.

A breeze is blowing over the ground, but it doesn't dispel the heat or my dizziness as I wobble out of the plane and take a look around. I'm anxious to speak with Dorothy, but something tells me to keep my distance, for now at least. I don't think she would be happy to discover that I had smuggled myself on-board her airplane...again.

Rounding the tail to get my bearings, I realize airplanes are parked in rows all around us, yet ours is the only that looks like Betty. Good, she'll be easy to spot. I'll just take a quick look around and come back, as this plane seems to be my transportation.

Single-engine flying machines with huge, round engines

supporting long propeller blades inhabit the rows nearest to us. Behind their great noses are long, narrow cockpits covered in glass. The planes are propped up on two hefty tires and lean back over a small wheel in the back. They remind me of lions resting on their tails, waiting to pounce into action and roar down the runway, chasing the wind.

I walk along the row of machines, checking each one out with inquisitive apprehension, as I have no idea where I am or what will happen if I'm caught investigating. Then I realize that this place is so full of activity, I may as well be invisible.

Men and women are sauntering toward the planes wearing packs hanging low on their backsides, strapped to their shoulders and thighs. They help each other onto the wings and climb inside their respective cockpits as more airplanes taxi past the front row and then swirl into a parking spot. It is organized chaos.

Two women pilot some of the airplanes, while others have a man and woman inside. All of them are all dressed the same. The men are wearing khaki uniforms, while the women sport oversized jumpsuits. The straps and pads clinging to them look awkward and uncomfortable.

I'm almost mowed over by a couple women heading for an airplane on the opposite side of the taxiway. If I hadn't heard their voices first, I would have mistaken them for men because both ladies are wearing leather caps with their hair tucked beneath the edges and flaps covering their ears. One of them pulls a pair of goggles out of her front pocket and wipes them on her pantsuit while the other zips up her heavy leather jacket. The coat is just like Dorothy's and bears the same patch on the left side, under the collar. It's that figure of a girl with wings, boots and goggles. It must be a symbol for these women. I wonder what it means.

The women vanish from my view, but their laughter carries through the air, to be usurped by engines thundering to life all over the field. Then the beasts taxi out in a line, preparing to take off, just as Dorothy had done.

Not far from the rows of airplanes is a large, white hangar

with the words, "Avenger Field," in tall letters across the front. Attached to the hangar is a tower with steps wrapping around the outside, leading to a windowed compartment at the top. Two men lean against the railing that circles the structure, talking and gesturing. There are large megaphone-like speakers hanging off each corner of the building. It's a good thing no sound is coming out of them at the moment, because they look like they could knock a person over.

As the steps of the tower meet the concrete below, there are signs pointing upward, "Director of Flight 2nd Floor" and "Chief Dispatcher 3rd Floor." Over a screen door at ground level hangs a sign reading, "Instructor Ready Room." Inside I see all men, sitting at tables and benches. Some are in colorful conversations; others are looking over paperwork. One man, wearing a tan shirt with the sleeves rolled up and his thick, black hair disheveled, says, "She would have bailed out if I wasn't there! We were yawing back and forth; she was having a whale of a time!" All the men around him laugh and try to talk over one another.

Two women sit on a bench outside, poring over a map. They're dressed in the same mechanic type outfit, with cushions piled next to them. One of the women has shoulder length, wavy blond hair and is wearing a dark red lipstick. The other has short, curly brown hair poking out beneath a hat, and she's tracing her finger over an opened map.

"Betty," the blond haired girl is saying, "you have to fly through the whole beam and make sure you hear the code change before you start your turn back. It won't make a bit of sense otherwise..."

The other woman shakes her head. "I know, but I didn't even hear the change over there. I felt like I was just flying back and forth, listening for the darned 'dash, dot,' but all I kept hearing was 'dot, dash.'" Stifling giggles, she continues, "When I turned, it got louder when it should have been fading away, Eleanor."

Eleanor bursts with laughter. "Land sakes, you really were turned around!"

A door swings open behind me and three other women walk out to join the ladies on the long bench. All appear to be in good spirits, greeting one another as they find a seat. The wooden screen door slams behind them and I casually turn around to peer into the room they just exited.

Inside, ladies are chatting quietly. Some are thumbing through notepads or studying paperwork. It's funny that the Instructor Ready Room reminds me of what Dad's hangar looks like on a Sunday, with all the pilots trying to top one another with brave stories of death-defying events. But the women appear to be more sophisticated than the men. If it weren't for the maps spread across tables and the silly outfits, I might think these ladies are meeting for afternoon tea.

Just as I'm pondering their civility, a snort of laughter erupts from the corner of the room and I peek through the dusty windows to see a small group of women against the back wall. Some have propped themselves on top of the tables, with their feet resting on the benches. Others are bent over in a fit of giggles. The character of the group, a lady with curly black hair smothered in a handkerchief, is crossing her eyes and making a silly face while throwing her arms around in the air. The other groups join in on the joke and someone shouts between chuckles, "No brains for *your* breakfast tomorrow, Marie!"

Hm, maybe they *are* just as loud as the boys.

I wish I could go in and sit down with them and take part in what's going on around this place. I want to get to know these women. Maybe it's an attitude, or the fact that they're flying those incredible airplanes, but this desert airfield is fascinating.

Voices grow louder behind me as a group of men crowd into the Ready Room and I'm reminded that I had better keep moving. Maybe I can explore for just a couple more minutes. Betty won't leave without me, right?

I traipse across the dirt road and step onto a narrow wooden porch of the building next door. The overhanging roof stretches along the entire length of the stretched building. The structure is of a simple design, with a flat top, swinging screen doors, and rectangular windows. It's painted a cream color with a stripe of blue around the bottom, matching the rest of the single story buildings that multiply into the horizon. Surely these are the same ones I saw from the air when Dorothy was flying.

As I approach the window, I notice several women sitting behind rows of long tables, taking notes. The speaker is shouting out various numbers as the women furiously scribble away and then pause to listen attentively. Mounted on a metal stand near the chalkboard is the forward part of an airplane engine. I can tell it's an engine because it is gigantic and looks just like the ones mounted on Betty.

The instructor points at the machinery and says, "explain the combustion process to me, Carol."

A woman wearing two low pigtails in her hair begins to answer and suddenly the instructor's eyes are drawn straight to where I'm standing. He frowns and I duck out of sight quickly. Did he see me? Why is it that no one else seems to?

I crouch and hurry past the rest of the windows until I can no longer hear the man's voice. At the opposite end of the building is another classroom full of women. They are seated at tables similar to the last class and each of them is sporting a pair of headphones. Some are writing on the paper in front of them, others are frowning at the floor or table, deep in concentration. One girl with short, dark hair has her cheek in her hand, like she's focusing on the sounds coming through the headphones. A man is seated casually at the side of the class, tapping out sounds on a machine. He has a square jaw and resembles an old photo of my grandfather. I stop to hear what he's conveying through the machine, but I can only make out lots of beeps and clicks. Could it be Morse code?

I'm compelled to keep walking, but I make a mental note of how to get back to Betty. I will leave soon, but I just need a few more minutes.

Stepping out into the road, the wind dances through my hair. It has picked up quite a bit since I climbed out of the plane. Sand is blowing everywhere and some of it crunches between my teeth.

I take cover next to an official-looking building with a sign that reads "Aviation" above its door. Stepping back to read the rest of the sign, I realize that the character from Dorothy's patch is mounted above the building. It sends a shiver down my spine to see the figure mounted here, just like the patch I have in my jewelry box far, far away.

In front of the building is a tall flagpole with two flags flapping in the wind that seems to be getting stronger every second. One flag is the American flag; another is just a plain red. What could the red one mean?

A number of cars line the lot on the other side of the structure and one of them is a long, beautiful turquoise-blue Cadillac. Its white wall tires and chrome hubcaps sparkle in the sunlight. I know it's a Cadillac because my uncle has a purple one just like it parked in his garage. He once drove my brothers and me around the lake in it, and I remember my hair blowing about wildly as I watched sailboats float across the deep blue water. It was fantastic.

Inside the official-looking building, a woman is seated behind a desk. A large, black telephone hanging on the rear wall catches my eye. It looks so old! My great grandmother had a phone like that in her house and even that one was used for decoration.

The woman doesn't notice me peering through the glass as she examines the paperwork, so I stare for a while, trying to figure out what is so different about her. She is neatly dressed, with a collared, short-sleeved sweater and matching blouse. Her black hair is swept in a perfect wave off her forehead. Stacks of folders are balanced on the edge of her desk and piled on top of two hefty filing cabinets behind her. It looks like she has a lot of work to do and she's got to be burning up in that office, wearing a sweater. I can't imagine that the fan in the corner makes a difference in this heat.

It's a strange feeling, walking around out here by myself, gawking at all the people. It's like watching a motion picture happening all around me. I keep waiting for someone to round a corner and shoo me off the set.

From this vantage point, I see rows of buildings to the right that aren't much larger than trailers. I'll just take a quick look and then make the trek back to the plane.

The sidewalk treads through dirt and scattered weeds and then encircles a cement pool resembling a fountain. The water reflects a cloudless sky and silver coins glisten from the bottom. It's a rudimentary wishing well. What a bizarre place for a decoration like this, a hint of joy in the center of such boring architecture.

I march down the concrete path as the wind lifts grains of dust from one side to the other. The small buildings appear uninhabited. No one is milling about outside, but airplanes continuously circle overhead at different altitudes, each one waiting for an opportunity to land and then takeoff again. I hold my hand over my eyes to block the glare of the sun and count at least five airplanes maneuvering around the field. Six. Seven. How can they possibly avoid colliding with each other? The most I've ever seen at Dad's field is two or three at one time.

The sidewalk leads to a pair of long buildings that face one another. In the dirt between the structures, a sign painted white with black letters reads, "Women Trainees Only In This Area." Come to think of it, I haven't seen any men in the classrooms other than the teachers.

I step cautiously onto the long wooden porch of the building to my right and peer in through the nearest screen door. The room is vacant, so I pull open one of the flimsy doors to investigate the interior.

Six cots with basic metal frames are scattered throughout the room. Each mattress is wrapped neatly in a brown blanket and topped with a single pillow. Between the beds are tall, wooden shelves, some with a rod at the top to hang clothes upon. Shoes line the foot of each bed and there are large wooden boxes beneath each one. The women must live here. It's tough to imagine, since the room is so devoid of personality.

Taped inside a shelf are two black and white photos. I lean in to get a look at the couple standing in front of an old truck and smiling into the camera, but I'm jolted back by the sound of footsteps and voices outside. I dive out of the room and hide in the adjacent bathroom. From this angle, I can still manage to see the front window of the sleeping quarters. One of the voices outside sounds familiar.

"I just don't understand why he couldn't fly with me again today," the woman says. "He was supposed to be my instructor this entire week, I thought. It doesn't make a bit of sense, Marion." The screen door slams loudly into its frame.

"Well, all I can say is, everyone who is anywhere near you two can tell that you're sweet on each other. Darlin', if you're not careful, the entire base is gonna catch on, and then it'll go straight to you-know-who," answers an unfamiliar voice. The lilt in her words enlightens me to the meaning of Southern drawl, as this woman definitely has one.

"Marion, that's not true! Don't even think that for a minute or I'll be kicked out of here so fast! Besides, what about all those fellows who flew in yesterday, claiming they were having engine trouble? They sure gave you a lot of looks!"

Between peals of laughter, the women imitate male voices. "I'll teach you how to fly, girlie, but we might need to stay a while! Have you got any extra cots? Oh, never mind, I'll share yours!"

The women chuckle for a while, and then the one with a Southern accent cries, "Dorothy, hon, I wouldn't go on about it if I were you. He probably had to work the link again."

Dorothy? I thought the voice was familiar!

"You mean he's working the torture chamber," Dorothy says, giggling. The two must be changing clothes, as I hear hangars clanging against the shelves.

"Oh well," says Dorothy, "I have to go back up there tonight, so I guess we'll just have to see if he can make it." Her voice gets closer to the bathroom I'm standing in and I duck out just in time.

"Wait a minute," Marion says, joining Dorothy in the bathroom. "Did you say you have a night flight with lover boy? Ohhh, they'll have a fine time with that one! Heck, none of the other gals have even flown that plane yet. All I can hope to get my hands on is that Bamboo Bomber!"

"Oh come on, Marion, don't be ridiculous! You'd better hurry up or we'll be late for dinner," Dorothy retorts and I hear the screen door slam again. There's a voice echoing over the loudspeaker. The sound is garbled from this distance, making it difficult to hear the announcement.

I push the flimsy screen door open and watch the ladies walk down the porch until they disappear around the corner. The woman on the right, the taller of the two, is definitely Dorothy, so I follow at a distance until they meet up with a larger group of women and fall into line, marching right toward me!

I look around, but there's really nothing to hide behind. I tuck my head down and keep walking as the ladies pass by, not even glancing in my direction. They march in perfect formation, with their eyes straight ahead and arms swinging in unison just like the military. I stand and watch them go by as an airplane lands on the runway and another circles behind it. I have to go and find that twin-engine plane now or I may never get home.

I make my way to the ramp as several airplanes are returning to land, one after another. Every single one is an older model, perhaps from Betty's time, but they are clearly well taken care of. There certainly aren't any high-winged Cessnas out here.

Pilots gather near the tower and, before long, another group is falling into formation. There isn't a man in the group. Only women, dressed in those large jumpsuits with thick belts clinging to their waists, holding the outfit together. Some have goggles across their foreheads; others are wearing scarves over their hair. But they all look forward and march past me, again, like I'm invisible. They are singing a song and getting louder as they continue down the road.

"Along came a pilot, ferrying a plane. He asked me to fly with him down in lover's lane. And I, just like a silly fool, thinking it no harm, cuddled in the cockpit to keep the pilot warm..." The women march right down the center of the road, singing and stirring up dust as they go. "Zoot suits and parachutes and wings of silver, too. He'll ferry airplanes like his momma used to do..." They keep singing until the last row has dispersed toward the barracks. Good thing I got out when I did.

I wait until the ladies pass and step onto the road to get back to where the planes are parked and a pickup truck with a giant front grill nearly flattens me. The huge, circular headlights are the first things I see as I jump out of the way. It's an old truck, more ancient than Dad's, with a heart shaped hood that curves down to meet a front grill big enough to squash me like a grape. It turns to park next to the big, white building and I notice that the bumper is a wide strip of polished chrome, and tall slabs of wood surround the rear bed. The driver leaps out of the cab and jogs into the hangar, totally unaware of our near collision.

As the shock wears off, I make my way to the row of airplanes that are still twitching from recent use. The planes seem smaller than the ones that Dorothy parked next to earlier. There's a long line of them, shining under the sun.

Where is the plane that looks like Betty? I have to get home before Mom calls Sunny's house to find out how things are going and I'm not to be found.

I cross to the opposite row, but I don't see the plane anywhere. Granted, I didn't pay attention to exactly where we parked. Now I'm wishing I would have. I walk back and forth, from one end of the line to the other, expecting the airplane to appear. What if I don't find it? Can I just find a place to close my eyes and then wake up back at the airfield?

On the third lap, I see a twin-engine airplane parked inside the big, white hangar. Is that it? I make my way over, weaving behind a couple of smaller planes and watching for anyone who might not want me snooping around.

As I get closer, a man comes from around the corner, shouting to someone behind him, "We'll have to take the navigation bay out, and put some seats in the back, Pat."

"Yeah, that can wait you know," hollers a voice from the rear of the hangar. "I'd rather get a handle on these engine problems. I don't need any more fires around here!"

"Whatever you say," the man mumbles to himself and rounds the wing of the airplane parked behind Betty.

It's the perfect opportunity to duck inside the rear door, so I do it and take a seat against the back wall of the plane. Any attempt to brush away the grime is futile. Everything is coated with a layer of the stuff, so I wedge myself between metal rails and close my eyes.

I'm just getting comfortable when I hear a click and the mechanic swings the door open, jumping backward on his heels when he sees me. "What in the Sam Hill are you doing in there, kid? You can't hide out in here!"

I sit up straight as an arrow and look to the cockpit for an exit.

"Hey, Patrick, there's a kid up here, taking a nap in your airplane!" The man shouts over his shoulder. I think fast, jumping for the door and falling out onto the floor. I scramble to my feet and hear a voice yell back.

"Is it Captain Anderson's son? He was out here…"

Now I'm running flat out. I look back over my shoulder to see the mechanic turning back into the shadows of the hangar, but I keep running anyway.

How did he spot me? More importantly, how in the heck am I supposed to get home now? I'll have to wait it out. I'll get away for a while and then crawl back inside when the men aren't around. But, it will be getting dark soon. Dorothy said she was flying again tonight, didn't she?

I look behind the hangar, hoping to find somewhere to hide out for a while. The flat-roofed building about fifty yards away has a door propped open by a large rock. I scan the rear of the large hangar, just in case the mechanic sent out a search party to find me. With the tall fence, the vintage airplanes, and the women in uniforms and marching, this airfield feels like the military. It must be a well-kept secret, and something tells me that kids are not welcome.

I peek inside and don't see anyone, so I carefully step into the doorway. My eyes take a while to adjust to the dim hallway with doors on either side. The immediate space is empty, but strange sounds emanate from beyond its walls. I move slowly down the hallway until a loud THUNK coming from inside one of the rooms startles me and I run to the dark end of the hall, pressing myself next to a door that is cracked open.

A man is speaking inside and his voice echoes throughout the hallway, competing with the rest of the sounds in the building. "Army 1-4-0-4, cleared to Houston range station. Maintain four thousand feet, advise when ready to copy hold instructions."

I tiptoe to the edge of the doorway and crane my neck to see inside. What a sight! There's a miniature airplane that looks like something right out of an amusement park. It's painted blue, with yellow stubby wings and a matching tail with white stripes. The front end is chopped off, but the airplane is actually moving! The plane tilts to the side and then straightens back to level.

"Army 1-4-0-4," the man says, "Hold on east leg of Houston range between the range station and a point four minutes east of the station until advised by Houston tower. Expect clearance at one eight one five."

The man is sitting behind a large table, donning headphones like the ones Dorothy gave me to wear when I flew with her. He has straight, dark blond hair sticking out beneath the headphones and thick, blond eyebrows. The man's left hand is clasped around a microphone, while his right hand turns a knob. A pole with some cables attached to it rises from the desk. It appears to be manipulating an object that is tracing circles across the desk, drawing something on the paper beneath it as the man hunches over, studying its lines.

"Make sure you're keeping just one needle width deflection, Eleanor," he says into the microphone.

Is he talking to someone inside that little plane? The whole scene is fascinating. I want to have a ride, too!

I watch for a while and then the machine suddenly stops moving. The man peels the headphones from his ears and then sets them down onto the wide table. As he flips switches, a noise draws my attention to the little airplane and the top lifts open to reveal a woman sitting inside the chamber. She removes her own headset and brushes her dark hair from her forehead to look at the man.

"Much better this time, Eleanor. You bracketed the beam pretty well considering the crosswind I gave you." Then he cautions, "Next time I'll be throwing in some rougher air and I expect you to handle the full let down without problems. You have some homework to do, Eleanor."

The sweet-looking woman grimaces and then tousles her hair, giving up on the wisps that are hanging into her eyes. "Alright, Captain," she replies, looking exhausted.

"You can climb out and we'll take a look at how your patterns turned out. I'd like to go over a couple more procedures…"

And I'd like to check one of those little planes out. I should probably stay hidden a little longer, right? What would it hurt to search behind the doors for an empty room with an airplane to try out?

My attention is drawn to the doorknob behind me that has just clicked and the door begins to open. I dodge against the wall, but the door stops where it is and I figure whoever is inside cannot possibly have seen me. A deep, growling voice carries out into the hall as Eleanor's instructor pulls the door to their room closed, perhaps to prevent interruption.

"All right, Rose, do you have any questions before we get started?" the man asks. He sounds official, speaking slowly and enunciating every word. "We'll begin with a pattern, just to get you familiar with the link again, and then we'll move right into intercepting the beam. This will undoubtedly be tougher than last time because you won't know where the station is. Just remember, keep the volume on the lowest possible setting, so that you can hear when the signal gets louder or quieter. We're going to keep working on it until you are flying the right side of the beam every time."

From this vantage point, all I can see are the man's polished, black shoes. I wonder how he can possibly keep them so clean with all the dust around here. My white sneakers are covered in dirt, just from walking around the field. He stands and I can see his neatly creased pants drape over the laces on his shoes. There's the same wide table with a light pole right in the center of it, blocking my view of his upper body.

"Are you ready, Rose?" the man asks, walking across the room and I dodge across the open door to try some of the rooms down the hall.

Nearly every door has the peculiar sound of the airplane moving around behind it. I listen as instructions are given to turn to 270 degrees, climb at 500 feet per minute, contact tower, etc. I don't know how the person inside that machine has any idea what they're doing. Maybe it's like a video game and there's a television screen inside, like the one where you can race a car around a track.

Finally, I find a door with silence on the other side. I turn the doorknob slowly and put my forehead against the crack, eying the room. It's empty! I dive inside and close the door behind me.

The room smells stale, probably because the windows are closed. But one of the little airplanes is sitting still with its side door wide open, inviting me to check it out. I look the contraption over before climbing inside. The plane is larger than I expected, but still awkward to climb into.

As I plop down onto the seat, my knee knocks against the stick poking up from the floor and I silently deal with the pain. The panel resembles Betty's cockpit, but it's much smaller and with far fewer gauges. There are twelve circles in all, staring back at me like I should know what the heck they're all for, but I don't.

The largest gauge looks like the one that Dad refers to as an attitude indicator. It's the same instrument he taught me to look at when I couldn't see over the panel, the one that represents the sky and the ground, with a tiny airplane in the center that climbs, descends, and turns through the unmoving horizon.

Another gauge is obviously an altimeter. It has the needles that point to how high the airplane is above sea level. And then there are a couple different compasses, an airspeed indicator, a vertical speed indicator, fuel and oil quantity gauges, but I'm not sure of the rest. How do I turn this thing on?

"I thought Betty Jo was my next lesson." A man's voice interrupts my thoughts.

I whirl around to face a dark haired man with intense brown eyes standing over me, frowning. He tilts his head and confusion passes across his face as he glances down at the clipboard in his hand.

"Uh." I scramble out of the seat and step out of the little airplane.

The man traces his eyes over my jeans and sneakers. "Why aren't you in uniform? You know you're not allowed to be in here by yourself."

I stare back at the man and at the open door behind him. Maybe I can make a run for it.

He picks up the pencil on his clipboard and looks at me suspiciously. "I'm afraid I'll have to report you, Miss…what's your name?"

"Um, I'm sorry, I thought I'd left something in this room," I say, looking at the desk for an explanation.

Without thinking, I grab a thin booklet sitting on the corner of the desk and hold it to my chest. "My notebook, sir. Sorry." The man is perplexed but slides out of the way as I sprint to the open door and nearly run over a woman who is on her way in.

"Golly, that was close," she says, looking into my face. Inches away, I could count the freckles dotting her nose if I paused for another few seconds. But I run instead.

I turn back to see the man staring at me, dumbfounded, as I disappear through the door. Then I jog down the hallway and burst through the door to the outside. I'm greeted by a dust storm brewing over the hot ground and fading light. No wonder someone closed the door, sand is blowing everywhere. Cupping my hand over my eyes, I see that the sun has lowered beneath the horizon.

I'm not sure which is more painful, the sand in my eyes or my stomach growling complaints over not getting food for several hours. What about the granola bars in my backpack…inside Betty…back home? I have to get home.

I go back to the hangar where I saw my plane and linger outside the door, listening for voices. It sounds like things have calmed down for the day, so I squat on the ground and peer around the corner, looking for Betty's look-alike. It's gone. No twin-engine planes in the hangar at all, from what I can see. Great. What do I do now? I knew I shouldn't have stayed so long in that building!

The smell of food carries through the air and my stomach grumbles as I search the ramp for my ride home. No luck. Where could the plane have gone in that amount of time? Is it flying? The bench in front of the Instructor Ready Room looks inviting, so I take a seat. My limbs are tired and aching and somehow I've managed to get sunburned. I'm so thirsty that I would drink from a river right now.

I lean back against the wall and notice that the wind has settled down and the sky is lit up like a wildfire. The few clouds stretching out over the desolate plains smolder like dying embers as the sun slides further away. Clouds fade into an indigo glow. I hear chanting and singing. It gets louder and then dissipates.

The day is winding down over the airfield, and what a full day it was. I didn't even do anything. Resting my head against the wooden siding, my eyelids fold over stinging, burning eyes. I wonder how my family will react to my disappearance.

Within a matter of seconds, the very bench I'm resting on becomes the center of activity on the airfield. I lean into the shadows as about a dozen men thunder down the stairs and enter the room behind me. Groups of women march out from between buildings and enter the Ready Room, where a man is erasing and rewriting names on the large chalkboard. Women crowd around him, searching for their names. Most of the ladies are dressed in the same baggy jumpsuits and carry those strappy seat cushions they all seem to have, but a few of them are holding leather jackets in one hand and goggles in the other.

Men and women break into pairs or groups of three as they leave the ready room for the airplanes parked nearby. Great! Maybe I can spot Dorothy and catch a ride home! Though I keep thinking that if someone gave me a cot and an occasional hot meal, I would stay here and learn how to fly these awesome airplanes. I'd do exactly what these ladies are doing. In fact, I would even scrub the bathrooms and wash all the dishes around here if someone would let me come back for flight lessons one day.

I recognize Dorothy's auburn-colored hair and her elegant gait as she moves across the ramp with a good-looking male instructor. He has deep-set eyes beneath dark eyebrows and a strong, angular jaw.

This is my chance. I can stay and most likely starve or get tossed out on my ear or I can jump in back of Dorothy's plane and hopefully get a ride home. Then, maybe I'll be able to convince Sunny and Karla to come back here with me. They would love it as much as I do. We could all learn to fly here!

Right now my belly is telling me that I need food and my eyes burn from lack of sleep. So I hop behind the pair and follow them out to the same twin-engine airplane I came here on.

Dorothy performs a preflight of the plane while the instructor climbs up into the cockpit. I creep along the tail section and wait until she rounds the right engine, and then I make my move. The darkness makes it easy to crawl inside the open door to the cabin, but I have to crunch my body into the very rear of the airplane so that Dorothy can climb up to the cockpit without spotting me. The operation is a success! Dorothy gets herself buckled in as she and the instructor discuss what will be covered in her lesson.

Before she starts the engines, Dorothy clears her throat softly and asks, "Is Instructor Moore still not feeling well, Captain?"

"Miss Morrow, you may refer to me as Hanson. And no, Moore is fine. He has been assigned to the link for the next few days. One of the fellas had to go home to his family and he's the only other person trained on it," the man explains.

"Oh." Dorothy sets her checklist to the side and leans her head toward the window. "Clear!" she yells out and the engine sputters, then kicks into a low roar. Dorothy fires up the second engine and proceeds to check out the various gauges. I move to the front of the cabin and lean against the panel that separates the cabin from the cockpit.

There's movement all around us as we taxi out to the runway, but we are the first of the airplanes to reach the end of the pavement.

Dorothy hesitates before continuing and I hear each engine grow softer in turn until they melt into one sound. She must be making her before-takeoff checks.

Dorothy turns us onto the middle of the runway, and it looks as though there are fires burning on either side of us. My eyes must be fooling me as I stare at the lights, moving by faster and faster until we lift off the ground and into the twilight sky.

The ride is bumpy on the climb out, but then gets smoother as we soar higher into the night air. The world looks lovely. I peer out the side window and see moonlight reflecting off the blades of the propeller. If I didn't know better, I would think that I was on a ride at the amusement park. Lights twinkle on the ground below. Families are probably getting settled after dinner, sitting on porches and visiting with neighbors; children are gazing up at the orange moon as it rises above the horizon. They are forming dreams as broad as their imaginations as they admire its magnificent glow.

I lean my head back and close my eyes and think about everything I've seen today. I smile as I recall the women laughing, the marching and singing, the lines of airplanes parked in rows and proudly pointing their noses toward the sky. And then I think of the sign that rose high above the plain office building, the one that matched Dorothy's patch from her jacket. Who are these women?

A hammer is pounding away somewhere...

Chapter 17: Troublemaker!

"Hello! Hey! What are you doing in there?" It's a man's voice, and he is angry. He is shouting in my ear. "GET out of there right now!" He is banging on the wall next to my head and shining a spotlight into my eyes. Where in the heck am I now?

Reality strikes and I fight to leap to my feet, but the sleeping bag confines my movements. I'm drenched in sweat and disoriented. I yank my legs from the flannel lining as my heavy flashlight crashes to the floor. It rolls away and bangs against the rear wall of the cabin.

The man begins to tug at the door, fighting the bungee contraption that is pulling it shut. "GET OUT OF THERE RIGHT NOW OR I'M CALLING THE POLICE!"

The police? I scramble to find the flashlight so I can get the heck out of here. But how can I escape? The man outside is blocking the door! I think fast as I notice that the hook on the end of the bungee cord is barely clinging to the metal ribbing. I scamper up to the cockpit, but the window is too small to crawl out. What about all my stuff? If I leave my backpack for the police to find, they'll be at my house within the hour. A vision of my mom, standing on her front porch holding my bag and surrounded by police cars, flashes through my mind.

"I'm calling the police, I tell you! You're trespassing, you know!" the man shouts again. The knocking has stopped and the bungee cord is tight again. I hear his footsteps moving away from the airplane. And then I see white hair glowing beneath a twilight sky.

It's Henry! Oh, no! What is he doing out here?

It must be nearly sunrise because a pink glow lights up the air. The fog makes it impossible to get a clear picture of the old man but his footsteps are scuffling away from the airplane, back toward his hangar, and I hear his heavy side door slam shut.

I move faster than I ever have in my life. I twist the bungee off the door and grab my backpack, stuffing the sleeping bag in as I run to my bicycle. I fight to keep everything inside the bag while balancing on the bike.

"Stop! You come back here!" Henry yells as I pedal as hard as I can, not taking my eyes from the path in front of my tire. I see much further anyway. Where should I go? It's too early to go home; my mom will know something's up. I have to go to Sunny's house.

My tire hits a rock on the side of the path and I'm airborne for a second. I skid across the dirt path, scraping my knee and elbow. The flood of adrenaline helps me pick up the things that flew from my backpack and climb back onto the bike. I pedal furiously until my lungs are heaving for air.

Getting some distance from the airport and Henry, I notice that the fog has dissipated. There's a pale pink glow touching the tips of the mountains.

I'm exhausted and weak from all the excitement and lack of rest. When I reach Sunny's house, blood is dripping down my forearm and the knee of my jeans is torn, exposing skin that is speckled with rocks and dried blood.

It takes a forever to wake her by tapping on the window next to her bed. By the time Sunny opens the front door, I'm ready to lie down and close my eyes in her front yard.

My friend pushes her tangled blonde hair out of her eyes and squints into the sunlight. It's clear that I woke her from a deep sleep. "Wow, what happened to you?" she asks, looking down at my arm. Sunny opens the door wide and I follow her in to the kitchen.

I look around the living room. "I didn't wake anyone else up, did I?"

She frowns. "No, I don't think anyone else is even home. Mom and Rick stayed with my aunt and uncle last night. Daisy might be here, but I doubt it."

"Did my mom call last night?" I ask.

Sunny shakes her head and smiles. "You got lucky." Her eyes drop to my torn jeans and bloodstains. "How did you get so torn up? You didn't actually spend the night out there, did you?"

"Sunny, you won't believe it!" I say, getting my second or third wind. "It was crazy! I saw Dorothy! I actually flew with her again!"

"What?" Sunny says in disbelief. "No way. There is no way that old airplane actually flew." She looks at my elbow and my jeans again and then studies my face. "Are you all right? Did you stay up so late that you're hallucinating? I've done that before."

I brush off the dirt on my pants. "No, I'm fine, I'm totally sane. I don't think I slept at all, though. And I have no idea where I was, but it was hot like the desert and I saw all these women flying these crazy airplanes and marching like the military. It was so cool!"

Sunny grabs two sodas from the refrigerator and hands me one. "You'd better clean yourself up before your mom sees you like that. Then you'll have to think up a whole new tale to tell." She tears off a handful of paper towels from the roll and sets them on the counter in front of me.

I crack open the soda and finish it in seconds as my friend watches me with a strange look on her face. It feels like days since I've had a cold drink.

It takes at least an hour to retell the entire evening's events to Sunny as I stand in her kitchen, scrubbing my wounds with paper towels as she sits at the long counter top in her pajamas, watching me in disbelief.

"I can't believe you actually did it. Karla and I didn't think you'd really go through with it! We were sure that you'd chicken out and end up over here." She fishes a powdered donut from a box on the counter and slides the box toward me.

It's the best donut I've ever tasted. "Is Karla here too?" I ask, excitedly. "I have to tell her what happened. She won't believe that I saw Dorothy again!"

Sunny shakes her head at me and wipes her face. "No, she couldn't come last night. But we should call her and have her come over right now," she says, reaching for another donut and scattering powdered sugar all over the counter. "Do you think that scary man knew it was you in that old airplane?"

I toss the towels into the trash beneath the sink. "I don't know. I hope not."

It's late morning by the time I hop on my bicycle and say goodbye to Sunny. I decide that it's better to get home early and have fewer questions from my mother.

The air is warm for being so late in October as I pedal through quiet streets. Rays of sunlight filter through tree branches as brightly colored leaves fall to the ground, gently gathering on sidewalks and in gutters. The weight of autumn hangs upon the sun as it begins to trace a lower path through the sky. Winter will soon take over the town. Snow will fall and turn to slush on the streets. Mornings will bring a pale blue sky with frost clinging to bare branches and straw-colored grass. White, blue and gold are the colors of winter here.

I pass a man washing his car in the driveway while his wife chases their toddler down the sidewalk. There isn't much traffic on the roads. It's feels like every other Sunday, quiet and melancholy.

I turn onto Mom's block to find a familiar truck parked outside her house. Ugh. It's Dad. Panic strikes and rises in my belly, pulsating out into my limbs. I slow down, thinking that maybe I can turn around and go back to Sunny's house and dissolve into her couch, but it's too late. Dad is sitting on the porch and he's already spotted me. I try to act nonchalant as I rest the bike against a tree at the end of Mom's driveway and wave to him.

"Am I staying at your place tonight, Dad?" I ask, swallowing my fear.

He shakes his head. "No. I've spoken with your mother and I've been waiting for you to get home so that I can have a talk with you, too." He pats the cement next to him. "Have a seat, Grace."

I can tell by the way he says my name that this is not good. He's not even smiling.

"Is everything alright, Dad?" I throw my backpack on the step below and the metal flashlight falls out, making a loud noise as it crashes onto the cement. I snatch it up quickly and shove it back into my bag, well aware of Dad's reaction.

He grimaces. "Since when do you take a flashlight with you to spend the night at a friend's house? And why are you so dirty? What, did you and Sunny sleep on the floor of her garage?" Dad doesn't allow me time to answer. "Now, I'm going to ask you a question, and I want you to answer honestly, Grace, got it?"

I swallow hard. "Uh…sure, Dad."

"Were you messing around at the airport last night?" He is watching my every move.

I'm caught. Any way that I answer, there is no positive end to this conversation. If I lie, he will know, and I'll be grounded for life at the very least. If I tell the truth, things could get even worse.

"Why would you ask that, Dad?"

"Well, Grace, it seems that someone caused a lot of commotion at the field last night. Henry thinks it was you and your friends who decided to spend the night inside that old Beechcraft and refuse to come out."

I can feel his eyes searching mine, but I cannot look at him.

"Grace, I told you that I didn't want you in there! He threatened to call the police on you!"

I sit quiet, but all I want is to run and grab my bicycle and ride far away from this conversation.

"Henry says this is the second time he's caught kids out at the airfield, leaving trash and breaking things, vandalizing…"

"What? Breaking things? I didn't break anything, Dad! What is that old coot doing out there anyway? Does he live in that stupid hangar?" I can't disguise my indignation.

"So, it was you?" Dad rubs his forehead with his hand and looks down at his shoes.

"Grace, Grace…Grace." He stops shaking his head and his eyes search mine. "Why did you go against me and lie to your mother? What possessed you to go out to that damned airplane in the middle of the night? What in the hell were you thinking? Did you know that the development company has been keeping an eye on the field; just waiting for something to happen so they can have the whole operation shut down, Grace? They can do that, you know. Report us to the FAA. Now, what would you girls do if you ran into one of those men in the middle of the night? How would you explain yourself?" His voice has risen in volume so that the last question is ringing in my ears.

Dad doesn't get mad very often, but when he does, it's scary. I stare back at him, but my voice isn't working. I want to explain the story to him, to tell him about Dorothy and all the old airplanes that I watched take off and land. I want to divulge everything, especially how I saw mostly women flying those powerful, enormous machines. And they were singing and having a good time all the while. But it's useless. He will think that I'm lying to him.

"Well, Grace, I've had it. If you refuse to listen to your parents, and you will not abide by our rules, then we have to get your attention some other way." Dad stands up and takes me by the arm. "Come on."

I look back and see my mom standing in the doorway, arms crossed tightly against her chest, glaring at me. This is the second time that I've seen her take Dad's side since the divorce. I like it better the other way.

"Well, move it, Grace. I have some things I need to give you and I don't have all day!" Dad pulls me along, leading me to his pickup truck, where there are two trash bags in the back. He lifts them out and sets them on the curb.

"This is all the stuff you had packed in that airplane. I don't have room to keep it at my house, and I bet your mom doesn't either. I suggest you donate it to the Salvation Army or throw it away."

He is leaning down so his eyes are looking down my nose, like my mom does when she's scolding me. His frown lines look like crevices at close range and I pretend not to feel the pain of his vice grip on my arm.

"I cleaned that airplane out this morning," he goes on. "But, Grace, you are going to go and scrub the carpet and polish the windows of that old plane, as well as the rest of the planes that Henry owns in case he has to sell them or haul them away if the airport gets shut down."

He releases his grip on my arm and I feel the blood surging through it again. This is ridiculous. "Dad, I could never clean all those…"

He interrupts me with a hand motion. "I have some things to take care of today, so I'll have to pick you up from school tomorrow and you can get started," Dad says, standing above me now.

I lift the bags off the sidewalk and cross through the grass toward Mom's door to avoid any further reprimand. I just want to crawl under my bed and stay for a year or so, until all this passes over.

"Grace, wait." Dad grabs me by the shoulder and frowns down at me. "I also want you to apologize to Henry."

"Apologize?" I say, surprised at the hostility in my voice, since my insides are still trembling.

"Yes, Grace, apologize. Henry owns that airplane now, and you and your friends had no business hiding out inside it, refusing to open the door."

"Dad, I wasn't trying to defy Henry or make you mad or anything like that! It's important, Dad, I just…I needed…" Then I lost my words again.

"I don't want to hear it," he says, raising his hand in the air again, like a stop sign in my face. "You didn't need anything out there. Now, I made it clear that you were to stay away from there and you didn't listen. Grace, you're lucky I'm not making you clean the whole damned hangar for Henry."

Dad waves curtly to Mom as she watches us from the doorway. Then he turns on his boot heel to face me again. "Actually, that's a great idea. Before you clean up the planes, you're going to help Henry scrub out that old hangar of his. That ought to keep you out of trouble for the rest of the school year. Then I'll think of something else for the summer." He walks around the side of his truck, yanks the metal door open and climbs into the cab.

"I'll pick you up tomorrow," Dad shouts through the open window, gritting his teeth on an unlit cigarette.

I cringe as I watch him turn the corner, knowing I have to face my mother's wrath now. As bad as Dad's is, it really cannot compare.

I push the front door open and carry the trash bags holding my belongings into my room. I can't believe Henry said that I was vandalizing things.

Mom pokes her head into my room and I prepare for the worst.

"Grace, I'm going to let you cool off for a while and then I want to talk to you," she says calmly and then she notices my shoes. "Don't you value anything I buy for you? How in the world did those shoes get so filthy?" she exclaims.

I apologize and take them off. I should have opted for the hiking boots.

"Did you sleep in a barn last night?" she asks, picking something out of my hair. "Go take a shower and get all that dirt off your face. And throw your clothes in the washer so they don't get the rest of the house dirty. I want you working on homework until you're finished."

Mom closes my door and I'm thankful for the excuse to end the conversation.

Halfway through chapter five in my history book, I realize that I haven't read a word when Mom taps on my door. She is standing in the doorway, watching me.

"Grace, I'm afraid that our divorce has been hard on you and I want you to talk to the school counselor," she says with her eyebrows lifted.

"Mom, I don't need the counselor. I promise, everything is ok."

The truth is, my parents were divorced long before they filled out the paperwork. Dad buried himself in work every day while Mom did all that she could to keep things under control at home. When they were together, which was inevitably at the dinner table, they would argue. The subject would start with money and evolve into just about everything else under the sun. After years of this, they just sort of built their own lives. I think my brothers and I had felt the storm brewing.

As Mom stands there studying me, I want to reassure her. I want to explain that it isn't that her parenting is lacking; it is just my curiosity. I had to go to the airport. I had to learn more about Dorothy and those women buzzing around the airfield, flying old warplanes. Besides, she would love to hear about Avenger Field and all the female pilots there, I'm positive of that.

Mom doesn't say very much at dinner. And by the time I go to bed, I'm so restless and over-tired that I cannot sleep. Maybe I need a snack. I remember the granola bar still hidden in my backpack. As I peel the wrapping from it, all I can think about is what happened last night. I'm exhausted and feel like I've been awake for two days straight, but the events replay endlessly through my mind.

I'm glad I went out to the field. Something strange happened to me there. I saw the most amazing things, and it wasn't a dream. I could feel and smell the world around me. Heck, I washed my hair twice and it still feels like it's coated in grime.

But I should have approached Dorothy and asked her where I was. I could have learned about the other women there and what they were all doing flying those old airplanes alongside her.

Chapter 18: Henry's Place

At 3:45 sharp, Dad's rusted pickup truck is parked in front of the school and he's waiting to pick me up, just like he said he would be. I barely have time to catch Karla up on my adventure before he gets impatient and starts honking the horn.

I climb into the truck to face my somber father. "Hello, G," he says, lifting his eyebrows. He turns up the AM radio and the news is muddled between static outbursts as we drive to the airfield. He's probably still upset from yesterday.

When we pull into Dad's gravel parking spot outside the hangar, I notice how distracted he really is. I follow him, watching closely as he fishes for keys in his pocket and lets me inside.

There's something off about Dad today. Even his hangar is disheveled. Clean rags that are usually kept folded and stored in a bin next to the office are piled in a wrinkled heap on the floor. Tools are spread across the picnic bench. The notes Dad writes to himself to prioritize his schedule sit piled on top of each other on the corkboard over the desk. Some have even fallen onto the floor. He opens the refrigerator to retrieve a couple sodas and the smell of rotten food fills my nostrils. He offers me one, but I decline, which is highly unusual.

"Dad, is everything alright? Has that Ted guy been out here again bothering you?" I ask, unable to pull my eyes from the mountain of trash overflowing the bin. It's an odd sight.

Dad picks up a sticky note that has fallen to the floor. "Oh, no. But they're just waiting for us to screw something up so we won't have a chance to fight back."

"What do you mean, screw something up, Dad? Like if there's an accident or something?"

He looks at me and catches himself, "not an accident. They just want the FAA to have a reason to fine us or take away licenses, something that would make us have to close the airport. But I'm taking care of things, Grace. I just need time…" He is cut short by the phone ringing loudly on his desk.

Dad picks up the receiver. "Hangar One. Oh, yes. Hello, Ted." The disgust is evident in his voice. "Tonight? No, I need more notice than that. Wednesday? I'll have to get back to you. Humph. No. No one is going to set foot inside this hangar if I'm not here, I'll tell you that right now. I still have a lease on this property and, unless I'm mistaken, they aren't allowed anywhere near here until a deal's been made, Mr. Skylar."

"Yes, I have the number and, no, I'm not changing my mind. You can call my lawyer. Fine." Dad places the phone back into its cradle and sighs loudly. Then he crumples up a paper on his desk and bounces it off the wall, where it falls beside the overflowing trashcan.

I just watch him. I don't know what to say to help. He steps out of his office, looking at me like he forgot I was here.

"You alright, Dad?"

He runs his hand through his hair and looks around the hangar. Then he nods to me. "It's a mess in here, eh?"

"Pretty much." I look around at the place.

"Oh, Grace," Dad says, "I don't think I can hold these wolves off any longer. I might have to close up shop sooner rather than later." His face contorts into despair, but he shakes it off quickly. "But I'll be damned if I'm giving up without a fight." He looks at me and forces a smile. "Alright, G, you ready to go?"

"Dad, isn't there something that you can do? Can we get more people to help us fight for the airport? I mean, you know a lot of people in town."

Dad shakes off my question and points at a bucket in the corner. "There's cleaning stuff in there, Grace. You carry that and I'll look for some clean rags. We'll head over to Henry's hangar and check in with him, see where he wants you to start." Dad looks at his watch. "I'm sure he's over there by now."

Terrific. I walk over to the bucket wondering how awful it will be to be alone with Henry in that scary old hangar. It's creepy enough with him three hundred yards away.

I trudge behind my father to the huge, white hangar, stopping for a moment to watch Jeff's airplane take off into the clear October sky.

Dad knocks on Henry's door until I begin to feel awkward standing outside. Henry's got to be inside. He always is. But I would be elated if he didn't answer.

After the third or fourth try, Dad cups his hands around his eyes to look through the smudged glass at the top of the door. I try to act indifferent, but I'm desperately hoping that Henry doesn't answer.

The sound of tires crunching gravel disrupts my thoughts. A blue Honda civic drives up and parks a few yards away. A woman with long, salt and pepper hair steps out and looks surprised to see us standing in front of Henry's door.

"Hello," she greets us. Her eyes are frowning but she smiles politely. "You must be looking for my father."

Dad steps forward. "Oh, of course, you're Barbara, right?" He reaches his hand out to greet the woman. "I haven't seen you in years."

The woman looks at Dad, puzzled. "I'm sorry, I don't remember your name..."

"It's Paul. I'm the mechanic across the field, and this is my daughter, Grace."

"Oh, right, yes. I'm so sorry," she says, waving her hand above her head. "I'm terribly distracted today." Barbara leans forward to shake my hand as well and I see that she has light blue eyes that sparkle like Henry's. But she looks weary.

"Uh, I guess you didn't hear the news about my dad." Barbara sighs and looks between us.

"No," Dad says, putting his hand on my shoulder. "Is everything ok?"

"Well...actually, he had a heart attack yesterday," Barbara says, fiddling with her keys.

"What? No, I didn't hear that. I'm so sorry, Barbara." Dad looks really uncomfortable now. "Is he...how is he doing?"

"Well, thanks, Paul. I'm sorry too," she says, looking at the ground. Then she smiles at Dad and looks at me like she's searching for words. "He's doing better now, much better than this morning. His neighbor's babysitter was leaving around midnight when she saw Dad collapse as he was climbing out of his car."

Barbara looks at Dad. "I have absolutely no idea what he was doing coming home that late." She shakes her head and pulls her hair away from her face, twisting it into a low bun. "Anyway," Barbara continues, "he's at Boise Center in town. He was in surgery for a couple hours, but the doctors say he did well and that he should be staying there for a few more days."

"Can we do something to help you?" Dad is pulling me closer to his side. "Grace was actually going to clean your father's hangar today, but we could help with something else that you might need."

She studies my dad. "Did you say you were going to clean?" Barbara asks with a laugh, looking at me now. "Heavens, no! You certainly don't need to do that, but thank you. I actually haven't been inside for years, but I'm sure that Dad hasn't stopped collecting old airplane parts. I'll bet it's pretty dirty in there."

Barbara steps toward the hangar door, thumbing through the keys on her beaded keychain. "I can only imagine what it looks like, really. And I have no idea how to find his paperwork and get everything together."

"Paperwork?" Dad asks with a frown.

"Well, since I'm his only child, I'll be responsible for getting his Will up to date. From what little Dad has said, I understand that he hasn't figured out what to do with all the stuff he's collected over the years. His home, his cars," she continues, making a grand gesture to toward the ramp, "and his airplanes."

Barbara must have noticed the frown on my face because she quickly clarifies. "I just mean that I should have come here to help Dad a long time ago, really. In case...well, something like this happens. You know, I suspected Dad was beginning to suffer from dementia after our last few phone calls. He would ramble on about seeing people that he'd known years ago. I should have come then." She shakes her head and looks at my father. "Have you noticed anything strange about him, Paul?"

Dad lifts his eyebrows like he's not sure how to respond. "No. Well, I can't say that I have." Dad looks at me for support and then says to Barbara. "Henry pretty much keeps to himself though."

Barbara laughs softly. "I know what you mean. Dad has done that all my life. Anyway, he doesn't really have any family left, except one older brother who is in a nursing home, and I bet the two of them haven't spoken in over twenty years. So, that leaves me to get things in order as best I can."

Dad exhales heavily, still holding onto my shoulder. "I don't know, Barbara. That sounds like an awfully big job for one person. Henry owns most of these old airplanes parked on the field."

"I know," she replies with irritation. "And I have absolutely no idea where to begin. Oh, and someone from a development company left me a message at the hospital. Do you know what that might be about?"

Dad sighs again. "Wow, they tried to reach you at the hospital? That's pretty brazen. It was probably the same man whose been pestering me."

Barbara looks questioningly at both of us.

"Was it Ted Skylar with Stonebrink Development?" Dad asks.

Barbara looks blankly back at Dad. "I'm not exactly sure, but that name sounds familiar."

"I'm betting it was. He's with a housing development company out of Denver that likes to tear up any land that's sitting near the mountains, so they can build homes on it," Dad explains. "They're trying to buy the property out here. I'll have to give you the number of the lawyer I use before you call him back."

Barbara looks flustered. "They want to buy the property? The whole airport?"

Dad nods and points toward the runway, "Yep. They want

to bulldoze the field and build a shopping center and a neighborhood right up against the foothills here."

Barbara studies his face. "You're kidding? Well, then. I would appreciate your lawyer's number." She hesitates. "What would that mean for you, Paul? If they did buy the land, where would you go?"

Dad shrugs. "We'll see. The fight isn't over yet."

"Hm, I'm sorry to hear that. Dad loves this little airport. I think fixing up planes has been the only thing keeping him active, really. And I bet you've invested a great deal in that business of yours," Barbara says.

"Yes, I have," Dad answers, sheepishly.

Barbara peers up at the white metal building spotted with rust and twists a key between her fingers. "Gosh, it has been a long time since I've been out here." She grimaces back at Dad and me. "You two are welcome to come in. I may be here for a while."

Dad looks at me for a reaction and says to Barbara, "Sure, we'll come in for a minute. Your dad did mention an airplane he's been working on, so maybe I can take a look and see if I can help him out with it."

Nosiness moves my feet to follow Dad inside Henry's hangar. It makes it even weirder to be here, knowing that Henry had a heart attack yesterday morning. Suddenly I feel compassion for the man who chased me out of the airplane and threatened to call the police.

"Oh, my." Barbara stops in the doorway and Dad almost bumps into her. "It's much worse than I thought it would be." She turns and faces my father. "I'm sorry, I really had no idea."

"Oh, we aren't worried about it," Dad reassures her. "Maybe it is a good day for Grace to clean up a bit." Dad must feel the fierce look I'm giving him because his eyes won't meet mine.

As I step inside behind them, I can see why Henry's daughter was so surprised. It looks like Henry tried to stuff three hangars into one. There are tools piled on each other on a long, wooden workbench. Several stacks of newspapers and magazines are scattered on the floor, some towering up to waist height. I can see the tail of an airplane, but there's a partition blocking my view of the rest of it and the divider is decorated with old photographs. They must be the photos I saw when I was standing on my friends' shoulders, peering through the window in the middle of the night. At least Dad never found out about that little adventure.

Barbara turns around and looks at me, then down at the bucket of cleaning supplies I am mindlessly carrying. "You don't have trash bags in there, do you?"

I sift through cleaning spray and de-greaser and shake my head. "No, just cleaning stuff."

"Well, Grace, I hate to ask, but as long as you're here, could you just take the top layer of dust off everything?" She waves her hands back and forth around her. "That would really help me a lot. Then I can see what I'm dealing with in here."

I nod to Barbara as she disappears into Henry's office and Dad peels off to look at the airplane hidden behind the entryway. My eyes trace over the seemingly endless piles of newspapers and magazines. From one corner to the next, the only spots without them are filled with tools or pieces of equipment taken off some sort of flying machine.

Take the dust off? This place needs to be sprayed down with a garden hose.

"Wow," Dad remarks, suddenly standing behind me, "it must have taken him decades to collect this stuff." He smiles at me for the first time in a while. The episode at Mom's house has taken a back seat to the news about Henry. "I appreciate you doing this, G," Dad says, walking back to the door and opening it so that sunshine floods in. "I'll be back in a bit."

The door slams shut, closing off the last whisper of fresh autumn air and replacing it with the smell of dust and oil. I promptly head outside to retrieve a rock and prop the door open with it. It's almost suffocating inside that hangar with the piles of debris lying around. I stand still, looking up at the sky.

The deep blue horizon is cloudless as the sun begins its descent toward the mountains. From Henry's doorway, I can see Betty. Material from her rudder is dancing in the light breeze. I imagine her as she looked when Dorothy was flying. Red and silver and powerfully beautiful.

I resist the temptation to throw my cleaning supplies in a ditch and go visit Betty, and slouch back inside the old metal building. I actually have to weave a path to the rear wall to reach Henry's workbench. Picking up the cleanest rag I can find, I start wiping off tools and organizing them like the ones in Dad's hangar.

After a while, my mind wanders and I sort through the nearest pile of newspapers. Wow. This one is eight years old, from Abilene, Texas. I lift up the paper and find another from 1966 beneath it, over twenty years old. Why would Henry want to hang onto these?

Ten minutes later, I've reached the bottom of the pile and found a newspaper from 1943. Unbelievable! These should be put somewhere where they won't disintegrate like some of them already have. The paper from 1943 has some sort of plastic around it, so it's thin and yellow, but the type is still legible. Amazing. What am I supposed to do with all this stuff? I can't throw the piles into the trash because they obviously mean something to the scary old man. Not only are the papers ranging in dates, none of them are from this area. Texas, New York, California, Arizona, how would one person acquire all of these?

Barbara walks out of her father's office looking exasperated. "Well, Grace, you certainly don't have to stick around." Her expression changes to disgust as she looks over the papers strewn about the floor. She tucks her hand over her forehead, beneath wisps of frizzy gray hair, like she's envisioning a world beyond this disaster zone.

"Ugh! How could my father possibly work like this? I should have come here a long time ago...and hired a cleaning lady." She smiles and weaves through the piles toward me. "Find anything good?"

I'm still clutching a newspaper from 1977 in my hand. "Your dad read a lot of newspapers."

Barbara reaches out to have a look at the paper I'm holding. "Hm, 1977? Why would he have a paper from 1977? Is there an article circled or something?"

"I don't know. I didn't look that closely. But there are even some from 1943 and 1944. A couple are like tissue paper, but some have stayed together," I say.

"What in the world?" Barbara looks at me with surprise and then studies the piles around her. "All these stacks are old newspapers? I don't know why I don't remember Dad stockpiling them. Seems to me he used to collect memorabilia and airplane parts."

I'm embarrassed at my lack of progress cleaning. "This is actually the first pile I've gotten to. I'm not sure about the rest of them." I point to the minuscule cleaning I had done on Henry's workbench. "I started over there, but…"

Barbara laughs and I can see the lines curl up beneath her eyes. "You didn't know where to begin. I don't blame you! Heck, I'm sorting through papers and notebooks that Dad has been stuffing into drawers for the past twenty years I'm sure! I cannot find a thing in his office either, except old photographs and some really beaten-up airplane manuals. He sure has plenty of those!"

Barbara's face completely changed for a moment when she laughed, like the weight of the world was lifted off her.

"Well, I'm going to get a couple things for Dad to sign and then I'm heading back to the hospital. Why don't you just wrap it up?" Barbara looks over her reading glasses at me. "I'm certain that a girl your age has much better things to do than clean a dusty old hangar." She smiles again and waves at a pestering fly, then walks back inside Henry's office. "But I know that Dad will be grateful for your help!" she shouts through the open door.

"Yes, ma'am. It will just take me a minute to stack these papers and finish the workbench," I say, eyeing the mess. Now that I'm free to leave, I want to stay and figure out why Henry has been accumulating all this stuff. I still haven't even looked at the airplane parked on the other side of the entryway partition, the one that caught my dad's eye. Then it occurs to me that I've really only seen a small part of Henry's hangar. The wall of his office must divide the building, but I don't see a door connecting to the other side. What was Sunny saying about the old man storing dead bodies over there?

With curiosity spilling over, I take my time leaving. Excuses race through my mind as to why I would need to stay in here longer without Barbara's supervision. I bet Karla and Sunny would want to take a look around too. Why would Henry collect these old newspapers and magazines? There must be a reason, other than kindling.

I gather the yellowed papers I had spread out and place them neatly back into a pile, and then make my way back to the bucket of cleaning supplies, stopping to peruse the photos on Henry's partition. They are all black and white. I've always loved the simplicity of colorless photos; so much is left to the imagination.

One is of a young man, grinning into the camera, with a little girl propped in his lap. The man bears a resemblance to Henry, though it's hard to tell for sure. It could be him as a proud father, showing off Barbara.

The next photo, another black and white, is of a small group of men. Some are kneeling, some standing, all gazing into the lens. They stare from a different time. The men in the front row are watching the photographer. Only a couple of them wear faint smiles, like so many of the black and white photos I've seen. In the back row, the men are beaming and gesturing to the camera. One man has his head back and I can almost hear the snort of laughter coming from him. The man at the left end of the row stands with his hand on his hip and looks faintly amused. He also looks older than the rest of the group, and a little like Henry.

The last photograph is of a woman, smiling shyly at the camera. She is familiar. As I lean in to get a better look, my heart drops. It cannot be. I'm looking at a photograph of Dorothy. Without a doubt, this is a picture of the pilot, the woman who handled that old twin-engine airplane in a storm with a dying engine, trying to comfort me all the while. She looks lovely. Her smile accentuates the dimples in her cheeks and her hair is curled just as I remember.

I don't know how long I've been standing, not realizing Barbara was talking to me, but I jump when she touches my shoulder. I turn to see her lips mouth the words, "Are you alright, dear?"

"Uh, yes. I'm sorry, I was...who is this in the photo?" I point to Dorothy and Barbara pushes her dark-framed glasses up to the bridge of her nose, squinting. I feel guilty asking a question that I already know the answer to, but I need some kind of validation.

"Oh, that's a woman my father instructed in the forties, during the war," Barbara replies. "Dad has quite a few pictures of her. I think he was fond of her. He hasn't ever told me that, but I've always had that feeling."

Barbara focuses on me again. "Most of these photos were taken before my parents met, and Mom really didn't like to talk about Dad's female students." She laughs to herself. "But if you ask Dad about them these days, he'll probably give you an earful. I certainly can't keep up with all the stories he has."

"Henry was her instructor? Did he...do you know her name?" I am studying Barbara now. I step back a little, trying to hide my excitement, but surely Barbara has some answers I've been searching for.

"Oh my, you would ask me that." Barbara loses focus on the photo and looks at the distant wall for an answer. "Is it Marie? No, Dorothy!" she says, snapping her fingers. "I believe her name was Dorothy."

There is one large butterfly spreading its wings in my stomach right now. I know that I have to speak to Henry. For years, I've feared the old man. Now he's the one person that just might understand me. Surely he'll have the answers to questions that have haunted me over the past couple months.

I thank Barbara and clumsily make my way to the door as the handle on the cleaning bucket slips from my hands and the contents tumble on to the floor. I nearly trip over the spray cleaner, hastily gather the supplies and toss them back in the bucket, making a grand exit.

I push open the door to Dad's hangar and find him sitting in his office, going through paperwork. "Dad, I have to visit Henry."

He tilts his chin down, studying my face. "What's the joke, G?"

"No, Dad, I'm serious. I really want to see him. Do you think you could take me to the hospital?"

"Grace, I don't even think the doctor would let us see him. I'm sure that only family is being admitted right now," Dad says, folding the paper he's reading.

"Ok, well, maybe we can pretend to be family." I'm standing in front of him in his office now, feeling desperate.

"Grace, lying is never a good idea. Ever. Do you understand me? Besides, I thought you said Henry was a creepy old man." He frowns at me.

I suppose he's right. I did say that. "Come on, *please*. I just need to ask him some questions about the stuff I saw in his hangar."

Dad isn't listening.

"Come on, Dad. I know you think I'm joking, but I think he knows the woman I flew with that night. The night you couldn't find me, remember?"

"Grace," Dad answers absentmindedly, "the man just had a heart attack. I'm sure he doesn't want to be disturbed or answer questions or do anything right now."

He sets the paper on a stack in front of him. "Why don't you get some homework finished?" He wheels his chair away and pulls open a drawer, fishing through more papers inside. "Your mom tells me that you've fallen behind in school, so I'm going to make sure you do some studying when you're with me. I'll cut you some slack on cleaning all of Henry's planes, but I'd like you to help with his hangar."

He slams the drawer closed and looks at me. "Why are you looking at me like that? I just need to take care of a few things before I get you to your mom's. This is important, G."

I slink down onto the picnic bench, wishing it were a Saturday.

Chapter 19: A New Friend

It is nearly impossible to make it through the school day. I think I've looked at the large, white clocks in every classroom a hundred times. Why does the second hand come to a stop whenever I'm sitting in this brick building? Is there some universal secret to slowing time so the teachers can stuff our brains full of dates and formulas and events that seem to blur when I read about them at home?

It doesn't help that a steady flow of questions about Dorothy kept me awake last night. I was trying to fill in the blanks, to piece together Henry's connection to the pilot. It's surreal to think that Henry knows her! Maybe he can tell me how it was that I rode with her inside that old airplane. I'm counting on Henry to have the answers to some of my many questions.

I made sure to ride my bicycle to school so I can stop at the hospital on my way home. But, as soon as the final bell rings to release us, I get panicky. The thought of speaking to Henry alone makes me shiver. Maybe I should swallow my curiosity and try to forget about these past couple months. No. I'm not giving myself that option.

All the way to the hospital, I think of how to word my questions. Surely Henry will want to talk about Dorothy. Maybe he can tell me about all the women I saw at that airport in the desert. He can tell me whether my mom is right about my overactive imagination.

I walk through the sliding doors of the hospital to find a receptionist sitting behind a desk decorated with fake flowers. It smells like Band-Aids and ammonia, and the same fluorescent light that illuminates the classrooms at school lights the sitting area. It feels industrial and cold, despite the couches and chairs decorating the space and the dim lamps in the corners. I sure wouldn't want to get stuck in here if I were sick. It reminds me of some of the horror movies I used to sneak downstairs to watch with my brothers.

I approach the desk and suddenly realize that I don't know Henry's last name. How will I ask for him? I search my mind, but the woman behind the writing table has set her pen down and is watching me, which causes my thoughts to go blank. She asks impatiently, "May I help you, miss?"

I clear my throat, and take a deep breath. "Yes, um, a man named Henry had a heart attack two days ago and, uh, I would like to see him, please."

The woman raises her thinly penciled eyebrows at me. "A man named Henry? Does Henry have a last name or can you tell me what room he's in?" She picks up the pen and scratches above her ear with it, waiting for me to answer.

Now I'm fighting for air. "Well, ma'am, can I use your phone to call my dad, please?"

"Grace, how nice to see your face here!" Barbara is walking out of the sterile hallway toward me. Her smile immediately eases my anxiety. What timing!

"Hi, Barbara!" I say, a bit overzealous. I had wanted to talk to Henry alone, but it doesn't matter anymore. Now I just want to see the old man. I can ask him about Dorothy while his daughter is in the room, right?

"I just came by to see Henry, if that's okay," I tell Barbara as I glance at the woman behind the desk who is blatantly eavesdropping.

"Well, Dad isn't saying much today. And he seems to be in quite a bit of pain. How did you get here, Grace?" she asks, looking at my backpack.

"I rode my bike from school."

"Oh my, you must be freezing. Can I give you a ride home?" Barbara looks sincerely concerned about me now.

"It's okay, it's on my way to my mom's house, so I thought I'd stop by," I say, shrugging off the attention. Honestly, I didn't notice the cold at all. I was too absorbed in my own thoughts.

"Well," Barbara says, studying my face, "I'm sure that Dad would like to see you, just for a few minutes. He really hasn't had any visitors."

I bet I'm actually the last person Henry wants to see, but that's not something I'm willing to admit to Barbara or the nosy woman behind the desk. I've made it this far; I will not screw things up now.

"Henry Moore, right?" The woman looks at Barbara for confirmation, then at me like I should know better.

Barbara nods. "Yes, that's right."

"It says here that only family can visit him," the receptionist says to me smugly. Then she shakes her thumb toward Barbara. "If she approves, it's alright this one time. I'll need her signature, of course."

Barbara looks at me and says briskly, "Ms. Olson, add Grace here to that list of family, please."

The receptionist frowns at me and then turns her chair around to face Barbara. "*Is* she family?"

Barbara doesn't flinch for a second. "Of course she is. Grace is Henry's granddaughter."

The woman sighs and crinkles her nose at me, and I feel my cheeks blooming with the blood that has just surged into them. Why would Barbara lie for me?

The receptionist pushes me a clipboard and points her long, red fingernail at the spot where I should sign, glaring at me as I do.

Barbara walks to the elevator with me. "Dad is in room 323. I'll take you up there, but I have to go and get some papers for him to look over and sign, so I won't be able to stick around."

"Thanks a lot, I appreciate it. You didn't have to..." I stammer, but Barbara raises her finger to her mouth to silence me.

"I'm afraid Dad doesn't have too many friends. It would be good for him to have a visitor other than me." Barbara smiles down at me. "It was nice of you to come."

We weave our way through the hallways, passing by windows that dispel the harsh lighting briefly. I see room 323 and I panic. What do I say to the old man? Is he going to know who I am? If he really saw me that night that I snuck into Betty, I may have contributed to his heart attack in the first place.

Barbara pushes the wooden door open and I'm taken back when I see Henry, lying still beneath a thin blanket, hooked up to machines that are beeping and flashing. He looks exhausted. And much older than he did the last time I saw him at close range.

"Dad," Barbara says softly, "you have a visitor."

Henry looks dazed, like the time I almost plowed him over outside his hangar. He was disturbed and talking to himself. Now he looks me over with those vacant eyes again, but, for a second, I see a flash of recognition.

"Hello, sir." No other words come to mind as I stare down at the old man.

Barbara reaches out and beckons me closer to Henry's bedside. "Dad, you remember Paul's daughter, Grace. She's the one who came over to clean your hangar." She looks at her watch and then at Henry and me. "Alright, well, I'm going to look for those papers in your office so I can talk to John. Then I have some things to take care of in town, but I'll be back in the morning, okay, Dad?" She touches his arm reassuringly. "Can I bring you anything from your house?"

Henry waves Barbara away, like the conversation is insignificant. She smiles at me and whispers, "Watch out, Grace, he's an ornery devil." Barbara smiles and winks at me. "Are you sure that you'll be okay riding your bike home? Can I call your father and have him come and get you?" she asks.

"No thanks, I'm okay," I answer, still staring at the old man who is mumbling to himself now.

Barbara smiles and leaves me alone with Henry. I step closer to the door, afraid of the old man's suspicious look.

Henry and I stare at each other for a while. I try not to show how nervous I am, but it's difficult to keep a pleasant look on my face in a room that smells like mothballs.

Finally, he says, "Well, spit it out, girl. You didn't just come here to watch me die, did you?" Henry's voice is quiet and raspy.

Stunned, it takes me a moment to form a reply. "What? No sir. I just wanted to, uh, stop by." This is probably the worst idea I've ever had. I compose myself and prepare to dash back to the elevators. "I'm sorry I bothered you."

"Well, don't you worry, I won't be chasing you out of any airplanes for a while, kid. That's for sure. Why don't you stay a while?" A glimmer of a smile passes across Henry's face.

His joking calms me down and boosts my courage. "I'm sorry about that night, sir. I just...well, I wasn't trying to cause trouble."

Henry nods and looks at the ceiling. I can see his chest moving up and down beneath the blanket. The room is buzzing with mechanical sounds, but feels painfully silent when no one is speaking.

"You've been seeing strange things, haven't you, kid?" Henry asks with a wide grin.

Goose bumps rise on my arms and prickle against my sweatshirt. Henry looks at me like he can read my thoughts.

"I'm sorry, what do you mean?" We both know that I'm hiding behind my words.

"Stop saying you're sorry! You came here for a reason, kid!" Henry yells out, and then is seized by a wheezing, coughing fit. He sounds terrible.

Listening to him, I feel helpless. I move toward the door to call someone in, but thankfully the old man calms down. I'm frightfully aware that I don't know CPR or how to call a nurse, other than by running through the halls, screaming.

"Damned tubes, putting things down my throat and making it so sore that it hurts to drink water...how am I supposed to stay alive like this? It's a damn shame that they can fix up my heart, but they can't do a thing to make me comfortable..." Henry is mumbling softly to himself and then stops abruptly, like he's just remembered that I'm standing against the wall.

"Alright, kid, take a seat or something. You need to settle down," he says, motioning to the seat next to him.

Instead I sit on the edge of a wooden chair in the far corner of the room, close to the door.

"I know why you're here," Henry says, watching me. "I saw your face when your dad pulled you out of that airplane. I saw the cut on your forehead. I bet you think I'm a senile old man, eh?" Henry asks, lifting his head off the pillow.

I shake my head. "No, sir, not at all. You're actually kind of intimidating."

He lets out a throaty laugh. "Well, I don't know about that." Then he searches for something outside the window. "You know, all of this started when I saw that BT-13 rotting on the ramp at that damned airport," he says. "I tell you, it was like looking at a red convertible in a black and white photo. It was alive, you know?" He looks at me, questioning.

I shake my head. "What's a BT-13?"

"Oh, it's an old training airplane from my aviation days. Heck, you've probably seen a couple of 'em yourself and didn't even know it." He squints his eyes at me. "Anyway, that plane reminded me of a life that I had walked away from. I had to have it, see. I wanted to buy it and polish it up, and see what was beneath those layers of wear and weather." Henry studies me.

"It was like someone had left it out there for just for me, knowing that I'd drive by and take a look. It was the very same type of plane that I trained those girls in."

I look at the floor, wondering if Dorothy was one of those girls. "What girls are you talking about, sir?" I ask.

Henry smiles mysteriously at my question, but goes on with his story. "I had just retired!" He is trying to shout over the hum of the machines next to him, but his voice only manages a loud whisper. "I retired from a stable job that had made me a lot of money. I had been away from aviation for almost thirty years before I happened to pass by that airport on my last day of work. My last day! And," he says, pointing his finger at me, "mind you, I had never looked back at those days! I had never questioned my decision to leave aviation until I saw that plane and it awoke something inside me that had been dormant for a very long time."

It's as though the man is speaking to someone other than me, and I battle with the decision to sit down or leave him to his memories. But something keeps me glued to my spot.

"Well, after I had...an experience with that old plane, shall we say, I proceeded to buy more airplanes. Oh, I was determined to find particular ones, see. A PT-19, a Piper Cub, I even found a P-51 that the owner practically gave to me." He scratches at the gray stubble on his chin.

"Then I unpacked my collection of newspapers and magazines and all sorts of memorabilia. See, something inside me had reawakened. I was beginning to feel closer to her. I wanted to see her, to remember that woman all over again. Then, you climb into the airplane that was sitting right under my nose, flown in by some hooligan and left to fade under the sun." The old man shakes his head at the ceiling. "And you discover the secret I've been holding onto for years! You met Dorothy, didn't you, kid?"

The goose bumps return and go all the way up my neck this time. I stare back at Henry. The old man that seemed helpless when I first walked in is looking strong now. He is aware of my reaction. He is watching my face.

"What? How did you know that?" I finally stammer.

Henry coughs and closes his eyes. "I just want to be out of this horrible place, with the bright lights and the bells and whistles." Then he opens his eyes and tilts his head down to focus on me. "Tell me about her, won't you? Tell me about how she looked when you saw her." Henry motions to the door. "Maybe you should shut that first."

I'm uneasy as I close the door and lean against the wall, giving Henry my full attention.

"I'm right, aren't I? Isn't that why you're here? Because you met the woman I've been thinking about for over forty years?" Henry is spry as a bird now. It is me who is cowering away in the corner.

"But, how would you..." I can't find the proper words.

Henry interrupts me with a loud sigh. "Well, kid, I'm

tired." Then he lies silent, pondering the view out the only window in the cold room. He breathes heavily for a while and I watch his face transform, as if he's sorting through memories. The man is quiet so long that I begin to wonder if he remembers that I'm standing here.

Finally, Henry holds up his finger and leans away from his pillow. "If anyone asks me to repeat what I'm about to say to you, I won't. I'll deny it to my grave, kid."

I nod back at the man, mesmerized by his warning.

"But I need to tell someone just like you do. I need to talk about it, get it off my chest as they say." Henry is talking, but looking through me, toward the window again.

I stand still, trying not to disturb this new flow of conversation.

"Over forty years ago, I had my own flight school." Henry hesitates, taking slow breaths as he speaks. "See, I had been flying airplanes since before I could drive a car. My dad had a friend with a biplane who earned lots of money barnstorming in his Curtiss Jenny. It was a pretty little bird and I thought it was the greatest thing I'd ever seen. The fellow's name was Arnold, but he was called 'Arnie the Ace.'" Henry chuckles and his eyes light up.

"Arnie was a spry little guy," he continues. "I had three inches on him and I was barely seventeen. Anyway, he would donate time to teach me how to fly. I think he owed my father because he kept landing on our farmland and offering rides. Heck, Arnie put on more than a few shows right next to our cattle yard." Henry smiles at the ceiling.

"But I have to admit that I've never been the same since I flew that old Jenny all by myself, way up in the air, looking over our cornfield. I could see into the next county." Henry closes his eyes, sifting through memories.

"Flying took my mind off my daily routine and all the chores that had to be done," the old man continues. "It gave me a feeling of accomplishment, greater than anything I had ever done. I had planned on attending junior college, but the flying sort of took over my life. I worked a couple of jobs through high school, saved enough money to buy my own plane and then I started offering rides and doing some barnstorming myself."

"Wow, you were a barnstormer? That's cool." I've read stories about the barnstorming days. It's wild to think that Henry actually was one of those famed aviators.

"I sure was, kid. But, before I could turn my head twice, I owned two airplanes and was running a flight school at an airport right outside my hometown. A fellow from Texas named Mitchell came to work for me as an instructor. We did all right, but it was tough to get people to pay for flight lessons back in those days. So, when Mitchell quit to go and live near his folks and teach cadets from the Army Air Forces to fly, he asked me to come along."

"The Army Air Forces?"

Henry looks at me like I've interrupted his train of thought. "Yes, the AAF, now known as the Air Force, but back then, they were part of the Army. We started training pilots before the US entered World War II. Anyway, it was a job that promised steady pay and help with room and board someplace in town," Henry says, looking me in the eyes. "During a time that gasoline was being rationed and I wasn't doing anything to help the war effort, I decided to close up shop and follow Mitchell to Texas. Why not?"

"So you moved with Mitchell to Texas? Did you join the military?" I ask.

Henry's looks pensive. "I couldn't join. As far as the AAF was concerned, I could teach in their planes, I just couldn't fly them in battle. I had some minor medical issues, see, and I was too old to be a fighter pilot by the time I looked into it. But I knew that I had to get out of my hometown and that I'd be helping the war effort, too. Besides, I was the only guy around that place without a wife or kids to speak of. So I moved to Sweetwater to teach young men how to fly. What I didn't know is that I was about to teach a bunch of gals instead." He smiles at me and raises his thick eyebrows. "Oh, I was terribly shy. Grew up on a farm out in the middle of nowhere and didn't date until I was in my twenties. Girls were intimidating."

"Anyway," Henry goes on, seemingly disappointed at my reaction or lack thereof, "I was in Texas for only a month when I heard that women were going to start flying for the military. As my luck would have it, those women were on their way to Sweetwater for flight and ground training from our group. Can you imagine? I guess the facilities in Houston couldn't handle all of them. There was one latrine and a line of ladies waiting for it most of the day." Henry laughs at this and then winces at the pain. I can see that he is struggling.

"Is that the button to call the nurse in, sir? I mean, just in case…" I point at a red button on the wall, uneasy about the look on Henry's face.

"In case what? In case I kick the bucket? Don't you call anyone! I don't need any more people poking around at me." He looks terribly uncomfortable, but I do as he says, keeping my distance from the bed in case I need to go and find someone to help the man.

Henry rests for a moment and his eyes close, but he fights to stay with the story. "I'd been hearing about these women, see. The AAF had a plan to train women to fly military aircraft so they could ferry the planes from manufacturing plants out to bases. I thought it was a pretty good idea because the demand for pilots was never ending. Lots of men lost their lives in that war, kid."

"My grandfather used to talk about the war and the friends he had lost," I say.

Henry nods, solemnly.

"Were the women training to be fighter pilots too?"

Henry smirks. "Nope. They were trained to do lots of things, but the AAF never intended those girls to go into combat, just wanted them to help out so the guys could go and fly overseas. It was a tough program and the ladies had to learn quickly or they'd wash out. Some of them ended up towing targets for shooting practice and would get accidentally shot at by soldiers on the ground. Others flew at night for searchlight training. They did all sorts of odd jobs, but mostly they ferried airplanes."

Henry pauses between sentences. "Boy, I'd been listening to the men complain about these girls for weeks. 'Why are these ninnies learning how to fly? That's a man's job; those girls need to be at home running the household! They're just going to make fools of themselves, these planes take muscle to maneuver!'"

Henry flashes me a mischievous smile. "But I was curious, see. I did go steady with one woman in my twenties, an old neighbor of mine from Michigan. Boy, did she hate airplanes! She broke it off with me because she said that one day I would kill myself in a plane and she'd end up a widow." Henry picks at a piece of lint on his blanket. "I suppose she spared herself from that tragedy." He tries to prop himself up against his pillow as his face twists in pain.

It feels strange to stand here and not be able to help the old man if something happened. I try not to stare, as he gets comfortable.

"Hand me that water, if you would, kid." Henry points to a plastic cup with a straw and I pass it over. "My throat is dryer than desert sand right now."

He draws the liquid into his mouth like a child. He must hate feeling helpless at his age after being so independent, after years of flying airplanes and living what seems like a wildly adventurous life.

"So, was Dorothy your student?" I ask, anxious to get to that part of the story.

Henry carefully sets the cup on the plastic tray beside him and then looks at the ceiling, rubbing his throat with a hand that looks like it's wired to twelve different machines. "She was." He nods, still looking at the ceiling. "I was in Sweetwater while they geared up for these women pilots, and I still remember the day they were supposed to fly into the field. The girls were bringing airplanes from Houston to this new training base and, ooohhh, boy, did that town go nuts. People were gathered outside, expecting the worst. They thought those planes would be crashing into each other, falling out of the sky, and who knows what else.”

Henry snickers. “No one guessed that they’d all make it safely, without incident, and they had some mighty fine landings, I might add.”

“I bet that was awesome!”

“I thought it was pretty darned exciting and so did the town of Sweetwater,” Henry smiles shyly. “After a couple of weeks, I was assigned some cadets and as I walked out to meet my first student, she’s doubled over, messing with one of the straps of the parachute hanging off her backside. Well, I just stood there watching and waiting. Finally I asked in a loud voice, ‘Dorothy Morrow?’ Boy, did she nearly jump out of her shoes! Heck, she stood straight up and her lipstick flew through the air, missing my forehead by an inch. I wasn’t sure where she had been keeping it, but I wasn’t about to ask, either.” Henry laughs which sends him into another brief coughing fit.

Caught up in Henry’s storytelling, I realize that I’ve moved into the chair right beside his bed. His voice is strained and I was having trouble hearing him over the worrisome coughing spells. Thankfully, he looks better after I pass the water closer and he takes a long sip.

“Can I get you anything besides water, sir?”

Henry shakes his head. “No, but you’d better start calling me Henry, kid.” He is practically choking over his words. “I haven’t talked about this in forty years. Give an old man a chance to get it off his chest, would you?” He smiles up at me. “Think of it like confession.”

Well, my Dad’s Catholic, but that’s about all I know about confession. So I sit, fumbling with a hole in the knee of my jeans until Henry swallows the last bit of water from his little cup and asks me to refill it in the sink. I comply and then take my seat next to his bed. I think we’re actually becoming friends.

Henry goes on, “so, I’m standing there, watching this woman with beautiful blue eyes and curly, dark red hair, tucking her lipstick into her oversized coveralls and I’m thinking, ‘Boy, what am I going to do with this one? She’ll wash out in an hour.’”

"Well," Henry says, "we made our way to the primary trainer and I supervised as Dorothy checked the plane over. Now, keep in mind," Henry looks intently at me, "I had watched her drop checklists and papers and nearly trip over her own shoes on our way out to the airplane. But as soon as she began to preflight that old bird, boy, was she meticulous. I mean she did not miss a beat. And she flew the same way, too. I never flew with a cadet, man or woman, who could fly better than Dorothy."

His words make me think of how Dorothy handled that large twin-engine airplane when I was her wing-woman. She was all business. It was like watching an athlete perform. "Did you teach her how to fly?" I ask, afraid of Henry falling asleep or forgetting his train of thought.

"Well, I taught her some, but she knew how to fly when she got there. She had already gone through the Civilian Pilot Training program and was working as an instructor when she got the letter from the Ferry Command. But she couldn't go to Wilmington when they first started recruiting because her mom was ill. So, when she got better, Dorothy headed to Houston right away." Henry looks at me intensely. "See, back in those days, people were dropping everything to serve their country. It was the right thing to do."

Henry sinks back into his pillow and is smiling again. "Boy, was Dorothy a pistol. That woman could always muster the strength to control those airplanes, no matter how much it took. Some had heavy flight controls; some took muscle to drop the flaps. And if you lost an engine on a twin, well, it took everything you had to keep it straight. No, Dorothy was slight, but she was powerful." Henry tilts his head back and narrows his eyes to peer over his nose at me. "You're a bit like her, I think."

I smile back and for the first time, I mean it. For some reason that I cannot explain, those words are very kind, not often given away by a man like Henry.

"So, what happened between you two?" I ask, pressing him to continue.

"Well, kid, as hard as I tried not to, even though my job was at stake," Henry looks like a child begging for forgiveness, "I fell in love with that woman."

I feel my cheeks get hot and I'm embarrassed that Henry is sharing so much. But I did ask, didn't I? I just didn't ask for those kinds of details.

"I looked forward to every day that I could share the cockpit with her. They were letting some of the girls check out in a twin-engine on the field, before the AT-17's started coming. I volunteered to instruct right away in that plane. I knew that if I trained her to fly a twin, why, it would take some time. But most of all, it meant that I could sit right next to her. I thought it was a perfect setup." Henry sighs. "I would steal glimpses of her whenever I could. I never really could get enough of that woman."

Apparently, the man has forgotten my presence. "Well, did she know how you felt, Henry?"

He looks up at me with sadness in his eyes. "It was forbidden for instructors to have relations with the cadets. Absolutely forbidden."

"So you never told her that you...cared about her?" I ask.

Henry is quiet. He closes his eyes and says, "I did tell her, kid. I stewed over it for several weeks. I tried to bury it all, but I knew that I would never get over it if I didn't tell her." He is lying still with his eyes closed now.

"Well, but, did you marry her, Henry?" The question is off my lips before I can stop it.

The old man is silent, like I turned off the switch that had been keeping him animated. Did the painkillers finally bring rest upon him?

Then I see the tears gently stream from his eyes. Oh no. This is not how I had planned our meeting to go. I stand up abruptly. "I'm really sorry, Henry. I didn't mean to upset you."

Henry blinks his eyes open again and looks at tiles in the ceiling. He motions for me to sit down.

I sink back into the vinyl chair.

"I did ask Dorothy to marry me, yes," answers Henry after

a long pause. "The night before she checked out in that twin-engine. See, I had fully planned to get her father's permission, and then formally propose to her after she had completed training and been assigned a base. I had all the details ironed out in my mind. But I couldn't risk losing her." Henry pauses. "Like I said, I was a thirty-five-year-old bachelor." Again, he looks at me like I should be flabbergasted. "That was a big deal in those days, kid."

I smile and shake my head, but it doesn't sound like a big deal, really. My dad's kind of a bachelor all over again.

"Anyway," Henry continues, "we had a night flight, just the two of us. I can still picture it perfectly. The moon was reflecting off the propellers. The lights from town glimmered in the distance and the stars were bright above us. It was the only airplane where we could sit next to each other, so it was a rare opportunity. None of the other girls that came after her flew the same twin-engine airplane that Dorothy did her training in. Some learned when they reached their respective bases, but a few never flew one."

Henry looks through me. "Anyway, that night, I knew that it had to happen in the sky; I had found the right moment. As she was rolling out of a steep turn, I told Dorothy that when she was done with training, I wanted to marry her, if she would have me. By then, we could do it without the military intervening."

"What did she say?" I prod the poor man.

"Well, she was laughing and crying and trying to control the airplane all at the same time. She leaned over and kissed me and I think we both forgot we were flying in a plane for a minute." Henry closed his eyes like he was seeing it again.

The nurse knocks lightly on the door and then pushes her way inside. "Oh, my. I didn't realize you were still here," she says, looking through her thick glasses at me and then down at Henry.

"You haven't been straining yourself, have you, Mr. Moore?" The nurse studies Henry, then says to me, "The doctor doesn't want him talking because he's still in a very fragile state." I can see that the woman's brown eyes are cold as she looks at me. She's even less friendly than the receptionist, probably because of the smell of this place, and perhaps the lighting. Maybe it's the sickness surrounding her daily.

I stand up from the chair, awakened to my surroundings and suddenly aware of the time, though the thought of sleeping in the vinyl chair and not going home to an angry mother passes through my mind.

The nurse looks at her watch. "Visiting hours are over anyway. You'll have to come back tomorrow."

I pick up my backpack and look at the poor old man lying in his metal-framed bed. "I have to go, Henry," I say, noticing how alone he seems and I wish I could help him. "I'm sorry if I upset you."

Henry shakes his head, but his pale blue eyes are pleading. "Why don't you come back tomorrow?"

The nurse looks surprised but watches me closely. I guess I didn't plan on my visit going this well either. I mean, wasn't it just days ago that Henry threatened to call the police on me?

"Yes, I'll definitely try to be here," I say, wishing the woman hadn't intruded on our conversation. She might be attempting to save his life, but his spirit is clearly fading. It feels awkward to hug the man, so I give Henry's hand a squeeze and depart the stale room.

Chapter 20: *What About Dorothy?*

It's another painful day of watching the clock and trying to survive science class. I'm having an extremely difficult time concentrating on what Mr. Rosenburg is saying. His monotone voice and overhead presentations make me want to climb though the back window and hop out onto the grass to make my escape. I keep thinking of Henry and Dorothy. What happened to them? Did someone discover their feelings for each other and turn them in? Who is Barbara's mother?

Finally, the minute hand reaches the bottom of the huge clock above the door and I tear out of class, heading straight for my locker. No time to catch up with friends today. On my way through the halls, I notice that it has started to snow outside. Oh well. The ride will be cold, but I refuse to go home without stopping at the hospital first.

I hardly feel the chill, though my cotton sweatshirt is no defense. I leave as fast as I can, to try to beat the storm. I know if I stick around the brick building too long, my dad will show up to throw my bike in his truck and drive me to Mom's. Any other day, that would be fantastic, but today I have a mission.

My face is numb and tears from the cold air have frozen to my cheeks when I arrive at the hospital. I fumble to lock the bike to the metal rack beside the entrance because my fingers aren't working very well.

The glass doors slide open and the hospital smell floods out. The heat feels good on my skin, so the two balance out. But my fingertips burn as they adjust to the air and I notice the same woman from yesterday sitting behind the "welcome" desk. Her thick, brown hair is teased into a nest and she is perched in her chair, watching me. It doesn't look like she's happy to see my face.

"May I help you?" the woman asks, like she has never seen me before.

"Yes. Room 323, Henry Moore please," I reply.

"Oh yes, you're his...granddaughter, is it?" The woman slides a clipboard toward me, pointing her long, red fingernail at an open line for me to sign my name while she scrutinizes my every move. "Visiting hours end at 6:30 sharp, just so you're aware."

I nod, adjust my backpack, and move past the reception desk as quickly as possible without running. I can just imagine the woman's fingernails clawing into my neck to question my relation to Henry.

The door to Henry's room is cracked open a few inches, but when I knock, no one answers. I slowly press on the wood and find a dimly lit room waiting.

It's nice that someone shut down the fluorescents. For the first time, I notice a lamp in the corner, offering warmth to the room. There are no visitors. Not even Barbara. I guess I wasn't expecting anyone, but I'm thankful for the chance to speak to Henry alone, just like yesterday.

He is lying still, with his eyes closed. Despite the soft light, I can see that Henry's face is pallid. Shadows exaggerate the purple skin beneath his eyes, making him look gaunt. I feel a knot in my throat building. Is this compassion I feel? I'm amazed at how much I've come to like this man over the past 24 hours.

I sink down into the vinyl seat next to him. The material is cold from the air finding its way through the windowpane. I sit for a while, thinking of what I could do to make the room less icy feeling. Flowers? A photograph? I should get that picture of Dorothy from Henry's hangar and bring it here.

There's a quick knock at the door and a nurse that I don't recognize peeks around the corner. "Well, hello there, I'm Jeannie. I'm just here to check up on Mr. Moore," she says, pushing a cart in front of her and parking it beside Henry's bed. She smiles at me. "You must be his granddaughter."

"Uh, sort of," I answer, fiddling with the straps on my backpack.

"Sort of, huh?" Jeannie studies me and then smiles. "Well, it's nice of you to visit, sort-of-granddaughter." She touches

Henry's wrist, feeling for his pulse, and then writes on her clipboard.

Jeannie looks to be the same age as the nurse I met yesterday, but much friendlier. Her blonde hair is pulled back into a tight ponytail and she moves through her duties with ease. "Did he just fall asleep?" she asks, looking down at my sneakers and then at my top, probably wondering where my jacket is.

I shrug. "I'm not sure. I just got here."

"Well, if he did, I'll probably wake him up with this stethoscope if I don't warm it up enough." Jeannie smiles, holding the instrument in her hand tightly. "Your sweatshirt looks wet. Did you walk here, sweetie?"

"I rode my bike," I answer. It drives me crazy when adults call me "sweetie." Somehow it is acceptable from Jeannie, though. I take it as an extension of her personality. No condescension there.

Henry's eyes flutter open as Jeannie monitors his breathing. "I told you. Darn it," Jeannie says with an apologetic look. "I tried to warm it up."

Henry is disoriented at first. He looks around the room and when he sees me, his eyes soften and his lips curl into a soft smile. Then he glances at the curtains covering the window.

"Hello, Henry," I say, smiling back.

"You made it, kid. Thought I might have scared you away." The old man's face gives a full smile and his countenance brightens immensely.

"Oh, I don't scare that easily, Henry," I say. "Besides, you never finished your story."

He laughs and the lines in his face soften. "It's been keeping you up, has it?"

The nurse looks at both of us and chides to Henry, "Well, it looks like you're still alive, Mr. Moore." She pats him on the arm. "We should be able to get you on solid food and disconnect all these little wires soon."

"Good thing," Henry coughs. "I've got a cab waiting

outside."

Jeannie laughs. "Well don't send me the bill!" She is still chuckling to herself as she pushes the cart out in front of her. "I'll be back in a while. You'd better still be here, Mr. Moore." Jeannie winks at me and leaves the door cracked open behind her.

Henry sighs and meets my eyes again. I wonder if he can sense my curiosity about his life.

"Didn't you have school today?" he asks, taking on a gruff tone.

"Yes, but I left right after. I was afraid I'd miss visiting hours," I say. Actually, I was terrified that I'd worn the poor guy out yesterday. I was hoping that Henry would have time to recover today and not get worse. Apparently, I had nothing to worry about.

"Well, you're going to have to remind me where I left off, kid. My memory is a little fuzzy these days." He toggles a switch and the head of his bed begins to rise.

"Wow, that's pretty cool, Henry. I didn't realize your bed could move," I say, watching the amusement on his face.

Henry smiles. "I didn't either until today. Jeannie's the one who showed it to me. I like her; she's another pistol, you know." He proceeds to raise the head so that he can look at my face without straining.

"You were telling me about that night with Dorothy and..." Abruptly, I recall the tears sliding down Henry's cheek when he spoke of marrying her so I interrupt myself. "You talked about what a great pilot she was."

Henry rests his head back to stare at the ceiling tiles. "Humph, I remember now. I guess I didn't finish the story, did I? Well, I may have left out a few things yesterday. Let me go back and fill in some of the gaps." He looks down at me and I nod my head and casually glance at the clock above his bed, anxious to hear everything before I get kicked out again.

"Well," Henry hesitates. "This is the part that I can't find an explanation for and you may be the only person on this earth who will believe me. But I will deny every word if your dad comes knocking on my door, wondering why I'm filling your head with nonsense, kid."

This sounds serious. "Ok, Henry," I say, pretending to zip my lips closed. "I won't say a word to anyone."

He fiddles with a Kleenex in his hand. "Well, I told you that I passed by the BT-13 parked out on the ramp on my way home, didn't I?"

"That's the old airplane, right?" I answer, remembering the story, but not the particular airplane. Heck, if it isn't an airplane that my dad has let me fly, then I won't recognize it by name.

"That's right. It's the same one I used to instruct the WASP ladies in."

"The what ladies?"

"Women Airforce Service Pilots. That's what the girls at Sweetwater came to be known as," Henry explains with irritation in his voice.

"Oh, ok."

"Anyway, after I retired, I was driving past the airport. In fact, I didn't even realize that it was an airport until I saw the basic trainer parked on the ramp. I tell you, when I saw that plane, my foot hit the brake before my mind went into gear. I had to stop. I had to go and take a look at the old bird. I hadn't seen one of those for a loooong time."

I nod, concentrating on Henry's words.

"Turned out the guy who owned it not only wanted me to buy the plane, he wanted me to take over his failing flight school. Well, I had done that before and I had no interest in going down that road again. But," Henry points at me with his index finger, "I left my phone number in case he decided to part with that old plane. Two days later, he called me with an offer that I couldn't walk away from. I bought the airplane and the hangar to park it in for a steal."

"Is that the hangar you have now?"

Henry nods his head. "Yes it is. But let me back up even more kid. Way before your time, and a few years before I moved to Texas, there was a program set up by the government to train pilots, called the Civilian Pilot Training Program. Now, the government was thinking that involvement in war was inevitable and the need for pilots would be great, but they didn't want to scare the public, see. So they paid colleges around the country to have flight-training programs, and they let one girl in for every nine or ten boys so no one would get suspicious. And the college down the street participated."

"Did they use our airport to train pilots?" I ask excitedly.

"Yes they did," Henry smiles approvingly at me. "I knew you were a smart kid. See, your airfield has some history. It has seen a lot more than you know."

"And people are trying to tear it down. They keep bothering my dad about it."

Henry looks sad when I say this. "I know. And believe me, I'm going to do my best to stop that from happening…bunch of greedy businessmen. I know the type too well." He pauses to drink from his water.

"Anyway, I won't bore you with a history lesson," Henry continues. "So I had this giant hangar, see, and suddenly my retirement had turned into restoring that old airplane. I worked on that bird day and night because, what the hell else was I going to do? The only family I had lived a few states away and I certainly wasn't going to leave Colorado just to sit in some nursing home and wait out my days near my daughter. She doesn't need an old geyser to take care of."

Henry looks down at his chest. "See, I had planned to travel the countryside, but when I saw that airplane, everything changed. It brought back all the feelings that had been locked up tight for years. Restoring it was more than just a hobby; it was healing some very old wounds."

Henry shifts in his bed, clearly uncomfortable and measuring his words. "Well, kid, one evening I was working on that old airplane pretty late at night, and something strange happened."

I sit staring at Henry, not about to interrupt.

He sighs heavily, "I had parked it out in front of the hangar because oil was seeping from seals and leaking all over, and making a real mess on the floor I had just painted. Now, I was in the back seat with my head buried beneath the instrument panel, reconnecting some wires, when out of nowhere a voice asks, 'Should I try it again?'" Henry looks at me with wild eyes. "I nearly had a heart attack, I tell you." He gasps for air and it sends him into a coughing fit.

I know the routine by now, so I reach over and push his cup of water closer to him.

"I looked up to see a woman, plain as day, sitting in the front seat!" Henry sips again and checks my reaction, like he's searching for doubt behind my eyes.

Satisfied, he keeps talking. "Boy, I didn't know what to do. I was sure that my mind was playing tricks on me because I'd been spending far too much time alone; working on that airplane, see. But all I could do was sit and watch this woman. She started turning switches and by golly if the engine didn't start up on its own, with no one out there giving it a crank!"

"You didn't recognize her?" I ask.

Henry shrugs and throws his hands up. "She was dressed just like the ladies I used to flight instruct in Sweetwater."

I take a deep breath and lean closer to Henry. Finally I find an adult who understands me.

"Not only did she start the engine, but she proceeded to taxi the airplane out to the runway."

"With you in the back?"

Henry nods and studies my face. "I didn't know what to do, kid, I was in shock over the whole damned thing!" Henry exclaims. "When I realized that we were actually moving, I tried to put the brakes on and they didn't work. I thought that maybe I'd torn out some cables somewhere, but then I remembered that the engine was shot too. There was no explanation for any of it. I suppose I could have jumped out, but I wasn't about to let her take off with my new bird."

"Wow, so did you fly?"

Henry's eyes are big and his pupils are so big that I can only see a faint outline of blue around them. "That old airplane flew. The woman took off, did some maneuvers and then came back to land just as the fog was rolling over the field."

"What happened after you landed? Did you talk to her?" I ask.

"Oh, I tried to, but I couldn't. She taxied in and parked the plane and after she shut it down, I jumped out to put the chocks in place. When I turned around, the woman had pulled herself out of the cockpit and turned the corner of my hangar, disappearing as quickly as she had come. Who knows how she pulled the chocks to begin with. It must have been when my head was buried beneath the instrument panel," Henry says, motioning with his hands.

"Hm." As much as I believe the old man, it's surreal to hear him tell such a tale.

Henry shakes his head slowly. "Kid, that airplane was in no shape to fly. The fuel had been drained from it for years, I had taken out the spark plugs, and how she got the darned thing started, well, it's a mystery to me. That night, I thought I needed to get my head checked out."

"That's like what happened to me in Beached Betty."

Henry looks at me, clearly confused. "Who?"

"The old Beech 18, the one that I flew with Dorothy in."

"Oh, yes, ok." Henry frowns. "I'll tell you what, kid, that night scared the wits out of me. I almost sold that airplane then and there. I even stayed away from the airport for a while. Took a break to get my head together. And if you tell anyone about what a crazy old codger I've turned into…"

"She had to be a WASP, Henry. Or maybe she trained here with the college."

Henry looks closely at me. "I don't know, but kid, when I saw your face that night that your dad's friend did a gear-up landing…I knew it had happened to you, too. You looked like you had seen something that most people never, ever see in their lives. Were you afraid?"

I nod. "A little. But, somehow I felt like it was all going to be ok, you know? Dorothy was a great pilot and somehow she reassured me."

Henry smiles. "I know what you mean." He pauses, reflecting on something. "I did have more experiences like that over the years, but never saw the same gal. I didn't know if the airport was haunted or the airplanes I was working on, or...maybe it was just me and my imagination."

"This sounds strange, but it became difficult to leave. Every time I went home, I felt like maybe I was missing an opportunity to see Dorothy again. I began to wonder if I could find a plane that Dorothy used to fly; if it could reach out to her somehow."

"Yeah, whatever happened with Dorothy? Did you marry her?" I question.

"Oh," Henry says, "I guess we didn't get to that." His face contorts and I can't tell if he's in pain or just sad. He clears his throat and looks up at the white ceiling. "Dorothy and I never married."

"Did the military find out and kick you out? Is that why Barbara doesn't know Dorothy?" I ask.

"Did you ask Barbara about Dorothy?" Henry asks, frowning.

"No. I mean, I saw her picture in your hangar and I asked about her. But it was because I knew she was the woman from my dream, Henry," I say, trying to explain myself.

"Humph." Relief passes over Henry's face. "Barbara wouldn't know Dorothy because I met Barbara's mother after Dorothy's accident. In fact, we married less than a year later. Of course, Claire left me and took Barbara with her when she was just a little girl. She blamed me for all sorts of things. But I think she just knew that I was never going to get over Dorothy. And I'm guessing that she didn't want to live the rest of her life that way. How could I blame her for that?" He starts to mumble, "...ran off and married a pilot friend of ours. I had to fight tooth and nail to get to spend time with my own daughter."

"Dorothy had an accident, Henry?" I ask, stuck on this sentence.

Henry breathes heavier now, like the room is collapsing on him. In his raspy voice he says, "Grace, I never married Dorothy because she was killed ferrying an airplane."

177

Oh.

The hospital room is blurred and colder than ever. This isn't the story I had expected. I thought they were torn away from each other by the war, or thrown out of the military because they had broken the rules. Not this. My mind is blank and both of us sit in silence.

"So, Dorothy...died?" I finally mutter, tiptoeing through emotions. "Well...what, how did she die, Henry?" It takes time for me to put the words together. The awkward feeling that I shouldn't be here, pestering this poor man, takes over again.

Henry wriggles in his bed. "No one knows exactly what happened, except that she crashed after takeoff. Her airplane disappeared into a low layer of clouds. Witnesses say they heard an engine sputtering, then the sound of the airplane plummeting into the ground."

Henry isn't fazed by my internal struggle; he's having one of his own. Powerless in his hospital bed, he studies the curtains hanging behind me. "Would you open those, kid? I wish they'd stop closing them. It's my only escape from these damned four walls."

I pull at the string on the side of the drapes, but it's stuck. So I push the curtains open from the center and we are greeted by a gloomy sky. Snow is still falling and the flakes are bigger now, but they melt as soon as they meet the concrete below.

We both sit and watch the snow fall from a darkening sky.

Then Henry breaks the silence. "It never made sense to me, kid. She was one of the best instrument pilots I'd ever seen. But, folks said the fog had rolled in; and the gal that departed right before Dorothy claimed that there was a thick layer of clouds she had to climb through. If Dorothy lost an engine in that, well, she'd have to react right quick."

The memory of that first night that I flew with Dorothy keeps flashing back into my mind. I picture her, confidently manipulating the airplane through a storm, losing an engine, and still getting us on the ground safely, in fog. How could she have crashed when she could clearly handle the plane so well?

Henry's voice is almost a whisper. "I spent a lot of

evenings looking up at the stars, searching the sky for a sign from Dorothy. I never could let her go, really. Claire was right."

I've been staring outside, thankfully, because tears are sliding down my cheeks. The emerald green curtains frame the gloomy October sky, reflecting the sadness in my heart over this woman I crossed paths with somehow. It's a strange feeling, but I feel a bond with Dorothy. I respect her. I look up to her, even though I have spent brief moments in her presence. Finally, I register Henry's last sentence. "Is Claire Barbara's mother?" I ask.

Henry purses his lips and nods. "She was a good lady."

I wipe my face and turn back to Henry. "I'm sorry, Henry. Were you at the airport when it happened?"

He shakes his head and starts coughing again, grabbing at his chest. He is wheezing between coughs, like his lungs are fighting for air. I stand and reach for the plastic cup, putting the straw to Henry's lips, but he is coughing too hard to drink.

"Should I call the nurse in?" I ask, ready to dodge out the door, if necessary.

Henry waves his hand with the IV needle taped to the back of it. "No...sit," he says in a hoarse voice. I watch as the poor man takes a sip of water and his coughing subsides. Henry clears his throat. "I was still in Texas when it happened," he says grimly, looking like an old man again. "They brought her body back to the airfield and asked for donations from the girls to ship her remains back home to her parents."

He rubs his hand across his forehead and over his eyes. "I tell you, that entire place was taken over by a sadness that could knock a person to the ground. Everyone was affected by the loss of such a sweet, wonderful lady. It was terrible, just awful. Not only were these girls, Dorothy's friends, asked to pay for her body to be transported, but the military asked for a volunteer to accompany the...her remains."

It makes me sick to imagine being that girl, bringing my friend's body home to her family for a funeral. I think of Sunny's mom, of Karla's parents, and how impossible that job would be.

"So I went to the powers that be and gave them all the money I had been saving for our wedding. I asked the Officer in Charge to give the girls their donations back, and then I nominated myself to accompany Dorothy's casket on the train ride home. I said that I could handle breaking the news to Dorothy's family better than one of her friends could."

Henry watches the snowfall with a resigned look on his face. "Besides, what did I care about my job at that point? I had lost the one person that meant the world to me."

"I'm sorry, Henry." I don't know what else to say. The only time I've known death was when a girl in my second grade class was killed in a tragic accident. Her name was Willa and I thought she was the kindest girl in our school because she always stood up against the bullies, like she had no fear. She protected the less fortunate kids and I admired her for that. I remember hearing about her death on the 5 o'clock news. It was a cold, overcast day. The sun was gone too soon and suddenly the oppressive grey found its way into our home and lingered there for days. That was the first time I had known loss. I still cannot fathom what Willa's family must have felt.

"Did you take Dorothy back to her parents?" I ask.

Henry closes his eyes. "No, and I've always regretted that. The officers pretended to hear my plea, but I found out later that it was all for show. They assigned one of the older girls the job early the next morning, before I could even catch wind of it."

Henry sighs and rubs his weary eyes. "The company wanted to cover up the fact that I had even asked. They suspected I had strong feelings for Dorothy, see, and I think the company wanted to fire me when I offered to take her body home." He shakes his head. "But I guess they needed instructors."

"Hm." I can't imagine his grief.

"The poor girl they picked for the task was Dorothy's roommate, Marion. She and Dorothy were so close. Boy, that must have been tough on her."

"Marion?" I ask. The name sounds familiar.

Henry nods and continues like he's seeing it all over again.

"I was glad to hear that Marion handled the job with dignity. The guys said she was very persistent in trying to get the AAF to give her a flag to drape over the coffin."

Henry looks at me to make sure I'm listening. "That's the way they did it for the men, you see. She wanted it to represent the service Dorothy had given to her country, of the sacrifice she had made."

"Didn't they give her a flag?" I ask, indignant.

Henry tries to answer but his voice seizes and he reaches the water before I can hand it to him. "The military didn't do it for any of the girls that I knew about. No siree, they weren't considered part of the AAF. The girls were still civilians in the eyes of the government, despite all the planes they'd ferried and all the other assignments they did right alongside the men, keeping an impressive record all the while. You know they moved more planes and had fewer fatalities, too?" Henry's face is marred with disgust. "Can you believe that? And not even a damned flag or a star for the family as recognition of their ultimate sacrifice?"

The whole thing sounds unbelievable to me.

"So, it was just Marion, accompanying Dorothy's remains. That poor kid had the whole train ride to think about the accident and what she would say to Dorothy's folks," Henry continues, picking at his blanket, "but word of Dorothy's death had already reached her mom and dad. They'd received the news by telegram."

"By telegram?" I ask.

Henry studies me. "I bet it's hard to believe these days that important news came by a few sentences, tapped out by a machine. And the darned thing said something like, 'Your daughter was killed today, where should we ship the body?'"

Henry looks out the window. "I heard about that years later. Boy, if I had known that back then, I'd have raised mighty hell. I would have been fired before I quit." Henry wipes a drop of water off his chin with his bed sheet.

I stew over his words. I think of the tiny cots with six to a room, of the heat and the dust storms spinning around that airfield. The women wearing oversized jumpsuits, leather hats and goggles in the scorching heat. They were living far away from their families, struggling to learn to pilot those airplanes, so that the men could serve their country overseas, battling an unimaginable enemy.

Though it seemed like the women enjoyed the flying, why did they have to fight so hard for a chance to stand alongside the men, sacrificing for their country? And then to die silently, with the public knowing nothing of their expense?

"How could the military get away with that?" I ask. "Did Dorothy's family ever know what she had accomplished or the powerful airplanes she was flying all by herself?"

"Oh, sure," Henry says. "Dorothy was close to her parents. She sent them letters about what went on at Sweetwater. She even told them about me." I see a smile wave across Henry's face and for a moment, he looks forty years younger. "But the military tried to keep a tight lid on the girls' flying expeditions. The press liked to tell stories about them, but women pilots didn't go over too well with the upper ranks...lower ranks either, for that matter. Eventually, that's what brought an end to the girls flying military airplanes."

"So what did they do, go home?" I ask.

"Yep. The last class of girls was told to pack their bags right before Christmas. In fact, the final WASP graduation took place on the third anniversary of Pearl Harbor," Henry said, looking at me over his nose. "It got mighty tough for them at the end, too. See, the AAF decided that they had all the young pilots they needed, so they just shut down the training. That meant that men like me, who were working as flight instructors for the military, were at risk of losing our jobs and being sent into active duty as foot soldiers in some foreign country."

"Well, lots of guys panicked. Heck, lots of their families panicked too. Folks were writing letters to congressmen, pointing fingers at the WASP women, claiming they were stealing pilot jobs from the men. And to top it all off, guys coming home from battle wanted those ferry jobs. They didn't want to have to go back to the battlefield in the sky, no siree. Too many pilots were getting shot down and killed or taken as prisoners."

"Well, what did you do, Henry? Were you afraid that you would have to go and fight?"

Henry frowns at me. "Heck no! All I could think about was Dorothy. I wished for any distraction from the terrible pain in my heart every day." He moves the head of the bed upward. "Kid, I was a fan of the WASP ladies. They had my vote. I didn't want to see any more of them hurt or killed, but I didn't want to stop them from flying and I couldn't have done anything about the press or the Congressmen getting all sorts of letters protesting the WASPs, written by worried family members. Reporters made it nearly impossible for the ladies to stick around."

"What did reporters have to do with it?" I ask.

"Well, these girls that were once portrayed by the media as brave women flying for their country were now being accused of stealing jobs from war heroes! The press changed their tune and the country bought into all the newspaper and magazine articles. Overnight, the girls were viewed as the problem instead of the helping hand that they had been for the past two years. It really was too bad."

Henry sighs. "So the WASPs disbanded and the girls were sent home. Many got married and had children. But, if I remember correctly, a few of them tried to get jobs with the airlines and were turned away, of course. That was when airlines didn't want anything to do with female pilots." As Henry speaks, I notice he is wheezing between sentences. He looks tired.

Now I remember Marion. "Henry, I think I actually saw Marion! She was with Dorothy when I snuck into the barracks!"

Henry looks at me and for the first time, I see surprise in his eyes. "Really? You were in the barracks, eh?" He leans forward and I can see the longing cross over his face. "Tell me about what you saw, kid. I need to hear what happened to you in that old airplane that night. Tell me more about Dorothy."

For the next half hour, I share the stories of my adventures with Henry. I tell him everything I can remember about the first night I saw Dorothy, about how she was so kind to me and how she handled that big airplane through the storm, setting it down with one engine. His eyes pull away from me, like he's picturing her face as I describe the encounter.

Then I share the story of the second time I saw Dorothy. Henry lies quietly, closing his eyes at times, but listening whole-heartedly as I describe the airfield with all the old airplanes parked outside. I talk about the buildings I saw: the classrooms with the engines mounted on the wall and the ladies listening to some sort of code, the miniature airplanes that the girls were using for training, and the barracks with the tiny beds and standing closets.

He smiles serenely when I speak about the flight with Dorothy, of how I sat in the back of the airplane and she turned and stalled and spun until I was nearly sick.

By the time I stop talking, Henry looks like he has fallen asleep. I had watched his eyes became lazy with every description of Dorothy, and now he is nearly unconscious. The memories must be soothing his spirit.

I slowly rise from my seat, realizing that I'm completely unaware of how much time has passed since I sat down with Henry. But before I can make another move, his eyes flutter open and he looks at me with warmth.

"You know, kid," he says, "you were at Avenger Field in Sweetwater, Texas. That's where I met Dorothy."

"Really, Henry? After listening to you talk about that field, I started to wonder if that's where I was. I sort of remember a sign with that name on it."

He nods, satisfied. "It was the very same one, kid. Don't know how you did it exactly, but you saw the very same airfield."

We sit in silence and then Henry says, "You know, all my life, I never believed in ghosts or aliens or anything like that. I had no reason to. Something changed in me when I saw that woman start up the BT-13. I must have passed that night over in my mind a thousand times, but I still couldn't tell you why it happened. I can only guess."

I study Henry's face, concentrating on his words.

"Over the years, I came to the conclusion that those women need to tell their stories. Their flying was cut short and the people that did know about their sacrifices quickly forgot about them when the military shut the operation down and classified a lot of the information about them. In fact, most people who lived through World War II wouldn't remember that they even existed. Everyone but them and their families, and maybe a few curmudgeons like me."

Henry looks at me intensely. "See, the moment I started rebuilding those planes, they began to come around, wanting to fly them again. It makes sense now that I would see them. I was there, you know. But, I'm not sure why *you* saw those women. I'm not sure why Dorothy came to *you*," he says, watching me closely.

"I don't know either, Henry."

"You know, kid, those women were alive and young and strong like you are. They were real. The airfield, the barracks, the airplanes, the people; all of it existed like everything you know to exist today. You were able to visit a very real part of the past. I have to believe you because I remember the place like it was yesterday. You describe it perfectly."

It's tough to wrap my mind around all this. It all is so surreal. Even Henry seems like part of my wild dream. "Maybe Dorothy was searching for you the whole time," I say, reasoning it out.

Henry smiles and his blue eyes are soft with kindness. "There have been times that I've felt Dorothy near. I even talk to the air, hoping for an answer; hoping to see her face smiling back at me. I wish I could touch her, you know?" He looks at the drawn curtains. "My heart has been searching for that woman ever since she died."

There's a quick knock at the door and it swings open. The overhead florescent lights flash back to life, blinding both

Henry and me. The nurse from yesterday pushes her cart around the corner and stops when she sees me sitting in the chair next to Henry.

"Well, well, well. I see you made it back today," she says to me, then turns to Henry. "You haven't strained yourself again, have you?"

Henry looks disgusted and asks the nurse, "Where's Jeannie? I thought she was coming back to check on me."

I stifle a laugh.

"No, she's with someone else, so you're stuck with me," she says.

Stuck is right.

I stand up, and look at the clock, feeling guilty that I've stayed too long again. Twelve minutes until visiting hours are supposed to end. Uh-oh. Mom is definitely sending out a search party.

Henry's hand grabs my arm and he looks up at me with desperation. "Not yet," he says, glancing at the clock. "Would you stay just a few more minutes, Grace?"

I slink back down immediately. I realize that it's the first time Henry has actually called me by name. "Okay, Henry."

I'm afraid that when I leave, I will close off all the information about Dorothy. Henry is talking about this now, but when we are at the airport, when I'm cleaning his planes, I'm afraid he won't acknowledge that we even spoke of her. I must be the first person he has told about Dorothy and his past.

Henry tries to speak and it sends him into another coughing fit. His breathing is heavy as he gasps for air between coughs. The nurse looks concerned and stops listening to his pulse.

"Mr. Moore," blurts the nurse, "I am afraid that you are finished talking for the day. I'm giving you medicine to calm you down and I'm calling the doctor in here immediately." Then she whirls around to point at me. "And you are going to have to leave."

I nod, thoughtlessly, watching her press a button on one of

the machines hooked up to Henry. Then she disappears out the door, leaving her cart behind.

Henry is still coughing and struggling for air. I reach for his cup, but it's empty. I dash to the sink for a refill and, by the time I return to his bedside, Henry has sunken into his pillow. He grabs my hand as I set the water on the table in front of him. "Grace, go and tell Jeannie to call my daughter. I need to see her. I want to see her tonight."

"Really, Henry? Tonight?" I ask.

"Yes. Tell Jeannie that it isn't an emergency, but Barbara needs to come as soon as she can, before I get shot up with all their drugs. My mind is clear right now and I need to talk to her." Henry says, "Jeannie will allow Barbara to visit with me after hours."

"Okay, I'll go and look for her. Is there something I can do before I leave?" I ask, feeling the coldness of Henry's hand still around my wrist.

His lips turn upward into a smile, but his eyes are getting heavy now. Maybe it's the stuff the nurse just gave him through the IV. Henry opens his eyes long enough to gaze out the window at the snow. The flakes have gotten larger. I watch them fall beneath the streetlights that have just illuminated. Cars have turned on their headlights and I think of the people behind the wheel, on their way home from work.

Expecting the nurse to return any second, I lean over Henry and squeeze his wrist before I have to go. I try to look reassuring, like people do when facing a person who is ill. I pretend that this man, my new friend, will be better in the morning. But he's clearly suffering in a way that I cannot mend.

"I'll just say goodbye...until tomorrow, Henry." I touch the man's arm and his eyelids wrinkle as he looks up at me like a child. Then he mumbles something I cannot decipher.

I lean closer, clasping his wrist. "I don't understand, Henry. What are you saying?"

He lifts his fragile arm and takes my hand in his. "Tell Dorothy...to pick me up in the C-45," he says.

I look at the man with uncertainty.

Henry motions for me to get closer. My cheek is so close to him that I can feel his breath. He whispers, "I believe you refer to her as 'Beached Betty.'"

Henry smiles at the recognition in my eyes and squeezes my hand. Something indescribable passes between us. I smile sadly and my heart sinks in my chest. Instinctively, I wrap my arm around his frail shoulder and hold onto the suffering man. "Goodnight, Henry. I'll see you tomorrow," I say, knowing that this may never happen.

I leave the room as the nurse is rounding the hallway with a woman in a long, white coat scurrying behind her. I deliberately avoid her eyes and look for Jeannie at the desk by the elevator.

No luck.

I try the other hallways leading away from the elevator until I find Jeannie standing outside another patient's room, speaking to a woman and a young boy. I stand at a distance, trying to get her attention. Finally, the woman's stare pulls Jeannie's attention in my direction.

She looks surprised. "Is your grandfather alright?" Jeannie asks.

"Yes, but he wanted me to give you a message. He wants you to call his daughter and ask her to come tonight. He says it's not an emergency, but I think it's pretty important," I tell her.

"Tonight? But it's getting late, are you sure he's okay?" Jeannie asks.

I nod.

"Alright, well, thanks. I'll go and check on him. Oh, and someone else is downstairs asking for his room, but it sounds like they might be looking for you. Is it your ride home, maybe?" she asks.

I nod again, absentmindedly. Oh, no. I just cannot bear the wrath of my father right now. I was looking forward to getting on my bike and pedaling for a while, even if it is snowing. My thoughts need to run their course.

I step out of the elevator feeling despondent and heavy,

thinking about what I promised Henry. How can I possibly get a message to Dorothy when I'm going to be grounded for the next...forever?

Dad is sitting on a bench in the lobby, pretending to read a magazine. Great, this is it. I'll never get to have another slumber party, go to a movie or get a license to drive. I give up.

"Hello, Dad," I say, expecting him to tear into me when he looks up from the car magazine. But he smiles instead, taking me off guard.

"Hello, Grace," he says. "Your mom called and asked if I picked you up after school. She said that you should have been home hours ago, and I told her I thought I knew where I could find you."

"Great. Is she mad?" I ask, wondering how she could extend my life sentence of being grounded. My phone and television privileges will be next to go. Surely I'll get to eat though, right?

"After I told her where you were, she calmed down. This nice lady at the front desk let me give her a call." Dad gives helmet head behind the desk a wave and she smiles back. Wow. I didn't know she could smile.

"Sorry, Dad. I had to come. I really needed to visit with Henry for a while," I explain, making my way toward the door. I didn't realize that I would stay this late without anyone knowing where I am. I thought Dad would berate me about my disappearance again.

"You don't have to apologize, Grace. But your mom was worried. You should have told her where you were going."

Dad tosses the magazine onto the glass table in front of him and stands. "Look, I think it was big of you to visit Henry. It's just a little strange because I know you haven't been all that fond of him in the past."

I want to tell Dad the reason I came to the hospital in the first place. But, when I think of what Henry said about denying everything and how the whole story would sound outrageous anyway, I clam up. My mind sorts through explanations, but I don't have the energy to lie anymore. And Dad wouldn't believe me if I told him how much I like the guy.

"Come on, G," Dad says, putting a hand on my shoulder. "Let's grab your bike and I'll drop you off at your mother's. I don't know how you didn't freeze to death on the ride here, but I guess you're as stubborn as your mom."

As soon as we're outside the glass doors, Dad looks at me and says, "Granddaughter, huh? What does that make me, Barbara's husband?" He laughs. "I never knew you were that close to the old man."

"What?" I ask, and then I realize what he means. "Oh, Barbara told her that. I guess she thought that Henry needed a visitor."

"Hm. Barbara must like you a lot."

On the way to Mom's house, Dad is just as distracted as I am. He smokes cigarette after cigarette and talks mindlessly about his neighbor who is apparently in one of my classes and has been building rockets as science projects.

I'm not really listening. But I'm glad he stopped questioning my sudden interest in Henry. And as soon as we park, I hop out of the truck quickly, hoping to avoid further conversation.

"Thanks for the ride, Dad. And thanks for not being upset."

Dad reaches down and surprises me again by giving me a hug before I take my frozen bicycle from him. Reading this as a good sign, I ask, "Can I go and visit Henry tomorrow?"

"Tomorrow?" Dad questions me with his eyes. "Tomorrow's Saturday, Grace. What's going on with you?"

"Nothing, Dad, but I'm staying with you this weekend, right? So maybe you can take me by the hospital?"

He nods. "Alright, maybe. Things are hectic right now so I won't promise anything, G. I have to get the guys ready for a meeting with the development company in the morning." He purses his lips. "And I need you to stay at your mom's until the meeting is wrapped up, and then I'll pick you up when I'm finished. I'll run you by the hospital if we have time, alright?"

"Sure. Thanks for the ride, Dad. I'll see you tomorrow." I

walk to the front door and we wave to each other as he drives away.

I open Mom's front door and am greeted by the smell of tuna casserole. I recognize the smell because she makes it at the end of the week, usually right before I head to Dad's house for the weekend. Probably because she's waiting for a paycheck and there is no other food in the house. I don't like to think of what she eats when I'm away. Toast or tuna casserole I'm guessing. One day, I hope to make enough money for Mom to have all the steak dinners she can eat.

"Hello," she shouts from the kitchen.

I yell back and make a beeline for my room to think about what just happened. But, as soon as I kick my shoes off and sit down on the bed, Mom is knocking on my door.

"Everything all right, Grace?" she asks, poking her head in to see my room. "I cleaned up in here so you can find the floor. It looks better, don't you think?"

I look around. Mom can clean my room like nobody's business. The bed sheets are fit so tightly that I wonder if I can pry my way between them. All my books are put away, no socks are on the floor, and jeans are hung in the closet. I can never make the room look this good, no matter how hard I try.

"Thanks, Mom."

She smiles. "Pick up your shoes and try to keep it this way. Dinner is ready."

I guess I will have to wait to process everything. Thankfully, it's Friday and I can stay up late with my thoughts.

Over dinner, Mom is in a talkative mood. She seems relieved that I was hanging out with an old man instead of a bunch of angst-ridden teenagers.

"It's really great that you went to visit Henry, Grace. I don't see kids spending time with older adults anymore," Mom says, handing me a napkin. "Henry's a good man."

I'm shocked. "You know Henry, Mom?" I ask.

She nods. "Of course I know Henry. I was married to your father when he started that business out there. I used to bring Henry banana bread on Saturdays," she says, sitting up straight.

"He was always so grateful. He loved my banana bread."

I'm watching Mom now. I wonder if Henry ever told her about Dorothy. "Did you meet Barbara?" I ask instead, testing the waters.

"Barbara is his daughter, right?" Mom frowns and looks at me for acknowledgement. "No, but I remember Henry talking about her. I got the feeling that they weren't very close. I think he missed her quite a bit." She studies my face. "Why do you ask? Was Barbara at the hospital?"

I nod. "I just wondered. She was really nice to me."

"Well, it makes me feel better that his daughter was there with him," Mom says, taking a sip of her wine. "I was worried that the poor man didn't have anyone. I thought of going to see him myself, but I wasn't sure if he'd remember me."

"Really? You were going to visit Henry?"

"Of course I was," Mom answers, like it's a silly question. "You know, I always felt sorry for Henry. I don't know if he had any friends or was really close to anyone. In fact, I never saw another person in that messy hangar of his."

"You were inside Henry's hangar?" I ask excitedly.

"Well, I didn't walk around inside or anything like that. I just stepped in the door a couple times. I never stayed. But I could tell that he was lonely."

Mom sighs. "I remember standing in the entryway and looking around at all these piles of stuff...everywhere. He had stacks of things all over the floor. And the dust! Well, you couldn't tell me that he was dating anyone if his hangar was that much of a mess. I imagine that his house is much, much worse," she says between bites of casserole. "I thought of offering to help him clean up the hangar, but I didn't want to offend him."

Mom proceeds to ask about what Henry and I had talked about for so long. I'm tempted to spill all the details, just because it's so much to handle right now. But how would she ever believe me? I'll have to call Sunny later and confide my secrets in her.

"Henry taught women how to fly military planes during

World War II," I reveal to Mom.

"Female pilots in World War II?" Mom asks. "I had no idea that there were female pilots back then. In the military?"

"Yes, Mom, Henry's stories about them are so interesting. They wore parachutes and goggles and these huge jumpsuits, just like the men, but they looked like Grandma. I mean, some of them were petite like her and they were flying these great big airplanes. The airplanes were a lot bigger than Dad's, like those planes from the old black and white war movies." I'm over-excitedly spewing out sentences.

Mom stares at me like she's suspicious of something. "Henry must have been feeling pretty good if he told you all those stories," she says.

"Well, he was coughing a lot and sometimes he would have to stop for a while, but when I offered to leave, he would ask me to stay. And he kept talking. It was so cool. Mom, it made me want to fly too. I want to learn how to fly the big planes, like those women did," I say.

She sets her fork neatly onto her plate and watches me closely. Then she takes a sip of wine, sets the glass down, and watches the red lines streak down the side of the crystal glass given to her by my grandmother. "Grace," she says, measuring her words, "that's a really tough career choice for women. Besides, flying those small planes to build up your flight time can be dangerous. You remember all those stories your dad would tell you kids? He has lost a few friends in airplane...accidents."

"I remember, Mom. But I also recall that you used to fly with Dad, and you said you loved it," I argue.

"I did. I absolutely did. Up until we flew through a storm over the mountains. We were lucky to make it through that, Grace," she says, pushing her plate away with food still on it, which isn't like her. "Another plane crashed into the mountains one week after we made that flight, in the very same area we had been flying."

This, I hadn't heard.

"And Grace, honey," Mom continues, "your father

practically lives out at that airport. It would be the same for you. Working through one license after another, building time, constantly looking for odd flying jobs."

"But, Dad said that I could build time in his airplane, so I wouldn't have to spend as much money on training."

"Of course he did," Mom says, clearly outraged by Dad's offer. "It's funny how he can offer so much help now, but he certainly wasn't around to help raise you kids." She throws her napkin down, picks up both our plates and disappears into the kitchen. Judging from the loud clanging noises coming from inside, I decide it's best not to push the issue. I gather the glasses and head in to help clean up.

After drying and putting away the dishes in silence, I head to my room to pack for Dad's house. Mom follows me out of the kitchen and we say goodnight early. She doesn't go to bed, though. It will probably be another night in the garage for her, working out her frustrations through stone.

I'm writing in my journal when Mom pokes her head in my door, wearing her sculpting apron. I was right. "You okay?" she asks.

I nod and scoot up to lean against the pillows as she sits down next to me.

"Grace, you can do anything you put your mind to. Anything," she says, looking at me intently. "Aviation is a long road and I just don't want to see you struggle. But, if that's what you want, far be it from me to stop you."

She laughs and pushes the hair out of my face. "You're as stubborn as both your parents, so even if I try to stop you now, you'll find a way to do it at some point."

"I don't want you to be mad at Dad," I say.

"Oh, Grace, don't be silly, I'm not mad at your dad. I raised you to have a mind of your own, and now you're using it," she says, brushing away my last words. "You know, you could do a report on Henry for one of your English essays. You could interview him about his flight-instructing job. I bet he'd like that and it would get you caught up in that class, wouldn't it?"

"I don't know, I guess so."

Mom gives me a peck on the forehead. "Goodnight, Grace. I'll be out in the garage if you need me."

She closes the door behind her and I stare at the ceiling, feeling restless. I let my mind trail off, back to Dorothy and the questions that have been repeating themselves in my mind. Why does no one else on the airfield know about her or Beached Betty?

It's after midnight when I climb out of bed, unable to doze off and forget about my discussion with Henry. Pulling apart the blinds to see how much snow has accumulated, I can hardly see into the neighbor's yard. A thick white fog obscures the world beyond my window. If not for the yellow patio light next door, I would have no depth perception into the haze. The light casts an eerie glow onto freshly fallen snow. I crawl back into bed and surrender to the fact that winter has arrived. I already miss the green trees and warm summer afternoons. I wonder if Dorothy ever flies that old airplane in the snow.

Chapter 21: Final Flight

Mom cooks breakfast for both of us and then busies herself with chores around the house. I finish cleaning my room and finally find an opportunity to call Sunny and tell her about my visit with Henry at the hospital. Quietly, so that Mom cannot hear, I tell her about Dorothy and Henry and how she was killed in an accident. She is silent.

"You believe me, right? I know this sounds pretty crazy," I say, afraid of her reaction.

"No, I totally believe you," Sunny replies. "It's just that, don't you know what this means, Grace?" she hisses into the phone. "It means that you can see ghosts! Dorothy had to be a ghost and you saw her and talked to her and now you find out that she died a long time ago. That's so unreal!"

"I know," I say, "but it really wasn't that crazy. She isn't like, scary or ghoulish or anything like that, she's actually really nice. She looks like one of those ladies from the old black and white movies! I want you and Karla to meet her. I think you need to fly with her too, it's so much fun," I say, remembering to keep my voice down.

"Grace!" Mom shouts from the other side of the bedroom door, and then pokes her head into my room. "Grace, I've been calling you," she says, realizing I'm on the phone and lowers her voice. "Your dad just pulled up."

I promise Sunny that I'll call her as soon as I'm finished visiting with Henry, and then I gather my backpack and extra duffel bag for the weekend. Dad is standing on Mom's entry mat, looking uncomfortably bulky in his winter coat. He and Mom exchange a quick look like I've interrupted their conversation and Mom turns away.

"Sorry I'm late, G," Dad says. "Are you all set?"

"Sure, Dad." I give Mom a big hug and she tucks a plastic bag filled with chocolate chip cookies into my duffel bag. I love when she does that.

"They're for later," Mom says, giving me a hug as Dad opens the front door.

"I'll bring her back tomorrow evening a little earlier than usual," Dad says as he holds the door open for me.

Mom nods.

I step outside and the cold air finds every part of my bare skin. The snow that fell last night has blanketed the grass and left the sidewalk wet. The mountains are perfectly clear and their white peaks glimmer beneath the sun. The sky is a light, powder blue. One would never suspect that fog had covered the town in the wee hours of the morning.

Dad opens the door to his truck and the heated air carries stale cigarette smoke in my direction. Resigned to taking the good with the bad, I toss my bags onto the long bench seat. Dad climbs in on the other side, reaching for a cigarette in his shirt pocket. I crack my window open in anticipation.

"I've been talking to Barbara all morning, Grace," Dad says. Something in his tone is foreboding. He rolls the cigarette between his fingers, studying it.

"Henry's daughter? Did the nurse get a hold of her last night? Henry asked me to pass along the message," I explain.

Dad looks across the cab at me. "She didn't mention anything about that, but Barbara did go and visit Henry last night," Dad says. Then he clasps my hand in his and I don't like the look on his face. "Grace, I'm sorry."

"Is Henry ok?" Panic rises in my belly.

"He passed away sometime in the middle of the night," Dad says with a heavy sigh. And then, letting go of my hand as though he doesn't know how to comfort me, he pats me on the leg and then turns the key in the ignition.

The truck rumbles to life as the heat from the engine pushes its way through the ventilation system. A giant piece of ice slides down the windshield, leaving a trail of water.

I don't want it to be true. I just saw Henry yesterday. I have a perfect picture in my mind of how his eyes sparkled when he told me about Dorothy. They were as blue as the sky. He was alive.

"I would have come earlier, but I was visiting with Barbara. She brought over some paperwork for me to take a look at," Dad says. "I'm so sorry, honey."

"How did he die?" I ask, attempting to swallow the tears that have already begun to spill down my cheeks.

Dad draws a long breath from the cigarette in his lips and the tip glows like an ember in a fire.

"Barbara said that he died in his sleep. She said it must have happened some time after midnight, because she was with him until then and he had fallen asleep. I guess she left when the nurse came in to check his vitals and the hospital called her at around six o'clock this morning." He flicks his cigarette ash out the window. "I feel bad for Barbara. That woman has been through a lot in one week."

"But was he okay when she left him last night?" I ask. "Henry told me to ask the nurse to call Barbara before I left."

Dad shakes his head and squints his eyes as he drags off the cigarette again. "Apparently so. I guess Henry wanted Barbara to come so he could talk to her about his Will. And she stayed with him for some time. She said that he had a lot of energy and his mind was clear, but that he had some things that he was eager to straighten out in case he had another heart attack." Dad looks out his side window, exhaling smoke as it billows through the cab.

I don't care about the smoke anymore. It feels like my head is sitting in one big cloud.

"Barbara mentioned that the doctor couldn't understand how the machine that Henry was hooked up to failed to alert any of the nurses on the floor. I guess the room was quiet when he came in to visit the poor guy. There should have been an alarm going off or something." Dad scratches his forehead and takes another drag off the cigarette.

The white haze in the cab reminds me of the fog last night, of Henry's last request.

"He died sometime after midnight?" I ask.

Dad nods, rolling down his window.

I don't realize that we're driving to the airport until Dad parks in front of his hangar. I sit, wondering if I need to go inside, wondering if I need to do anything at all. It's a strange sensation that has taken over my body and my mind won't accept the news about Henry. I had no idea that he was such a kind, interesting person until the last few days. But I cannot describe how much I have enjoyed his company; his raspy voice recalling memories that would be unbelievable had I not experienced what I did. I liked talking to the man. I was looking forward to hearing so much more. And I still have so many unanswered questions. I feel guilty that I never got to pass along his message for Dorothy.

Dad is standing, holding the door open for me to step out of the truck. "Come on, Grace. We have to talk."

I really don't want to talk about anything right now, but I follow as he unlocks the door to his hangar and swings it open for me to enter. My limbs are moving, but I have no strength. The picnic table looks good, so I make my way over and set myself down like a rag doll.

A mountain of papers is piled onto the corner of the table in front of me and I look around the hangar, realizing that it is a complete mess. Magazines and books are stacked on the bench beside me. Dad turns on the light in his office and I see more of the same. It looks like someone tipped over a magazine rack onto his desktop. The scene is so puzzling that it makes me forget about Henry for a moment.

"Geez, Dad, what happened in here?"

He is listening to messages on the answering machine in his office. He turns up the volume on the last one and a man's voice echoes through the hangar. "Yes, this message is for Paul Markham. This is Richard from the Government Publications office, and I just wanted to let you know that the records at this location only date back to 1950…" Dad erases the message and interrupts the following one, clearly frustrated. He paces inside his office, then retrieves a couple sodas from the refrigerator and sets one in front of me. Mom never keeps soda at her house, and the sugar sounds wonderful right now.

"Did you say something, G?" Dad asks, looking perplexed.

"I was just wondering where all the magazines and books came from," I say. The more I look around, the more shocked I am at how disheveled his hangar is. It's even worse than the last time I was here. There are tools lying around, an extension cord stretched across the floor, dirty rags still piled throughout the place like anthills.

"Magazines?" He follows my stare into the office. "Oh, those. I picked them up from a friend. I'm, uh, researching something."

"What are you researching?" I ask.

He doesn't respond and my thoughts wander back to Henry. My heart sinks.

"Grace," Dad wakes me from my thoughts, "tell me again what happened to you that night Karl landed with his gear up."

I frown at Dad, perplexed. This is what he wants to talk about right now? "You already asked me about that night, Dad. Remember, you didn't believe me?"

Dad smirks. "All right. Well, try me again. I'll keep an open mind."

I sip from my soda and argue with myself over how to tell the story to my dad. I have to stick with what I said before. "I don't know which part you want to hear about. It was a strange night, I guess. I must have, um, fallen asleep in that airplane and the next thing I knew, I was flying in the back of it with a lady named Dorothy," I say, feeling guilty about leaving out the details.

"Dorothy, huh? You remembered that her name was Dorothy? Did you talk to her at all?" he asks.

I frown at him. "Yes. Why are you asking me about this now, Dad?"

"I'm not sure how to explain it, Grace. I know this is a tough day for me to ask you questions like this, but I'm trying to make sense of some things. Barbara showed me a photograph belonging to her father and it made me curious. I should have gone to see the old man." Dad looks weary. "Anyway, can you tell me about your dream again? As much as you remember?"

I sigh and take another drink, contemplating sounding crazy all over again. I figure I have nothing to lose, so I spill everything that I can remember about that night. Dad listens while pacing back and forth in front of the picnic bench, one hand running through his hair and the other holding his soda can.

When I finish talking, he stands there, staring down at the pile of paperwork in front of him. "Grace, your story stirred up something in my mind and now I just don't know what to think."

"What are you talking about, Dad?" I ask, feeling uncomfortable. He is always rational. I don't like this scatterbrained version of him.

"Well," Dad sighs, "I never said a word of this to anyone but Karl." He pokes at a magnet on the refrigerator. "When your mom and I were going through the divorce, I was spending several nights on the couch out here at the hangar. It was a rough time and I wasn't getting a lot of sleep." He hesitates and then continues, "But some strange began to happen. And at the time, I explained them away, telling myself that it was all the stress taking a toll on me."

"What strange things, Dad?" I ask, instantly curious.

"Let's see," he says, sitting on the corner of the table and folding his arms across his chest. "There were nights when I was awoken by the sound of airplanes, loud airplanes, flying around the field. It would become so obnoxious that I would finally get up and go outside to see what was going on." He stops talking and tucks his head into his hand.

I don't say a word.

Dad looks up at me. "And every time it happened, the field was immersed in fog, so I couldn't see what was going on up there. I mean, Grace, I could hardly see the beacon. It was as hazy as the night Karl landed, the night you disappeared. I don't know how Karl even found the runway that night."

"I know, Dad. Dorothy and I saw the runway at the last second too."

Dad looks at me, his eyes trying to read something in mine. "Grace, was Dorothy a WASP?"

"Yes! Dad, she was a WASP! Henry was her instructor! He told me all about her and he said he wanted to marry her but she was killed in an airplane crash!" I blurt out, like I'm finally confessing the truth about some lie I've been telling. I take a deep breath. "How did you know she was a WASP, Dad?"

He stands up and acts nonchalant, but his hand is lost in his messy hair. "Oh, forget it. I think I'm losing it."

"Dad, what did you see?" I persist.

He begins to pace. "Well, Grace, something else happened and I remembered it after you told me about your dream. I was out here on the field late at night, trying to get some work done. I was looking through some manuals when I heard a noise outside the hangar. It was loud, like metal scraping on cement. Thinking I would catch some teenagers pulling a prank, I threw open the hangar door and found Henry standing outside, next to an old airplane. I had to stifle a laugh, but he looked very serious, like he was lost. When I asked him if he was all right, he started rambling on about the old plane and how he wanted me to take a look at the engine." Dad sits back down on the bench and rolls a pencil back and forth between his fingers.

I sit watching him in silence.

Dad's eyes meet mine. "I don't know how he did it, G. I could barely push that thing into my hangar. And after I got it inside, I tried to make small talk with him, but he just waved me off, saying that he had work to do. He said that he would pay me when he picked up the airplane." Dad shrugs. "He didn't seem concerned about what I would charge him and I didn't know what to think of the whole thing. Grace, when I opened up the cowling to look at the engine, I couldn't believe what I saw."

"What was in there, Dad?"

I watch as he digs his thumbnail into the pencil now. "The engine was gone, G." He laughs. "I don't know what Henry wanted me to do to that airplane, because not only did that thing need a whole new engine, it needed an overhaul. The ailerons wouldn't move, hydraulic fluid was caked on the sides of the tires, and I doubt if any of the instruments worked at all. I mean most of them were missing anyway."

"Was anyone out there with Henry?" I ask.

Dad's looks at me and I can't tell if it's the lighting or his face has gone pale. "Well, G, it's funny you should ask that," he says, standing up again and clutching the pencil. "When I was checking out the plane, I had this weird feeling that someone was watching me. I glanced over my shoulder and saw this woman standing by the door to the hangar, the side door, you know? She scared the heck out of me."

"Hm. What did she look like, Dad?"

"Oh, I don't know how to explain it. She seemed different, I guess. She had on a leather cap that pilots used to wear a long time ago and she had goggles strapped to her forehead. Her clothes were real baggy, too. It looked like she was wearing that old jumpsuit I wore when I worked for Don. And she was carrying a pack that looked like a seat cushion. She was raring to go, alright."

"She was a WASP, Dad, she had to be! It might have been Dorothy looking for Henry!" I jump up and lean over the picnic table.

Dad shakes his head, taken back by my enthusiasm. "You said Dorothy was in your dream, right? This is all too weird for me, G."

I grasp the seat of the bench and try to sound calm. "Okay, Dad. What did the lady say to you?"

"I don't remember exactly. But she did ask how long it would take me to repair the plane. I know that. And I told her that it needed more than what I could do in a month. Then I asked if she was Henry's friend."

"And?"

"She said that Mr. Moore was one of her instructors, but that she was getting checked out by someone else. Then she told me that she could fly the airplane just like it was."

"Her instructor? Dad, Henry was an instructor in World

War II."

Dad shakes his head. "I don't know what's going on around here."

"You saw a WASP, Dad! Is that what you're doing research on, those ladies?"

Dad starts to pace again.

"Did she say anything else to you?" I ask, trying to get him to talk again.

"I thought the boys had set up the whole thing to play a prank on me. So, I kneeled down to put the cowling back on and I shouted to the woman that she had a good sense of humor. And when I looked up she was gone!"

I sit down on the picnic bench and put my head in my hands. "Why did you never mention this before? Like when I told you about Dorothy?"

Dad looks at me like I should know better than to ask such a thing. "I couldn't tell you. It still could have been the guys setting me up, you know. She never said who she was, G."

I stare at my shoes. Dad is a non-believer. The picture of Henry drifts back to my mind and I find myself swimming through that lonely feeling of loss again. I wish it were summer. The trees would be full of green leaves and flowers would be blooming in gardens throughout town. The air would be warm, and my grief would be easier to deal with.

"Come on, Grace. Barbara wants to meet with us. She's over at Henry's hangar," he says, interrupting my thoughts. Dad picks up a set of keys sitting on the picnic bench, next to a stack of paperwork larger than my biology textbook and walks back to the side door, holding it open for me.

"Barbara wants to talk...to us?" I ask, following him outside.

As we walk across the ramp to Henry's hangar, I look at Beached Betty. She sits imposingly in her corner, not a hint of snow on her wings. It must have melted in the sun.

Dad knocks at the metal door and Barbara greets us with bloodshot eyes and a tender smile. She beckons us inside. Stacks of newspapers are still piled all over the floor. The smell of dust and mothballs permeate the air. But the fact that Henry spent so much time in here makes the place endearing.

"Thank you for coming," Barbara says. "I found a couple chairs if you wouldn't mind coming into my father's office to sit down. We can talk in there."

I look at Dad and he puts his hand out, indicating that I should go ahead.

If the hangar seemed messy, it is no match for Henry's office. The far wall features a wooden desk with a small upper drawer and two larger drawers on the side. The desk is supporting so many manuals that I am afraid it might collapse onto the floor at any second. A tiny television set sits on top of a stack of manuals.

Next to the desk are two file cabinets piled on top of one another and nearly covered in reminder notes. Most of them have numbers written on them, but a few are mentions of past events. There are bookcases lining the rest of the walls, and the shelves are packed with manuals and flying books. One entire bookcase is dedicated to magazines. No wonder Barbara felt overwhelmed sitting in here.

She takes a seat at the desk and I make my way to the chair in the corner, leaving Dad to sit in the middle of the crowded space.

"Well, Grace," Barbara says to me, "I'm sure Paul told you that my father passed away this morning."

I nod. "Yes. He did. I'm really sorry to hear it."

The woman smiles and pulls her hair off her shoulder. "Thank you. This week certainly has turned my life upside down." She smiles through teary eyes. "This is the first time in a long time that I have truly wished for a sibling."

Dad smiles back at her warmly.

"I'm sure glad you gave me your lawyer's phone number, Paul. He's already been very helpful and patient," Barbara says, leaning over some papers on the desk.

"I'm glad to hear that. John's a good man," Dad says.

"Yes, he seems to be. So far, he really has come through for me," Barbara answers.

I'm beginning to wonder why Dad and I are sitting here. It feels awkward to be interrupting this woman while she's grieving.

"Well, you two," Barbara turns to face Dad and me, "John still has to help me with the details, but he said that I can give you the information I have thus far."

I look at Dad. His face is expressionless.

Barbara sighs and looks between Dad and me. "Basically, my dad willed his hangar and all his airplanes to the two of you."

Dad's mouth opens and I can see that he wasn't expecting this news. "What? I don't understand. His hangar?"

Barbara laughs. "Yes, Paul, you get to take on all of this," she says, putting her arms wide.

"There must be a mistake, Barbara. We're all leasing this space out here," Dad says.

"Well, Paul," the woman raises her eyebrows, "my dad was quite a businessman. When he decided to buy the airplane sitting outside this hangar, he made a deal to buy the building too. He never liked to rent anything. He probably told you about the airplanes he bought when he was young."

Dad looks befuddled but Barbara keeps smiling.

"Dad said you'd be shocked at the news. You see, Paul, Dad paid fees to utilize the airport, but he said that he bought in at the right time. He purchased the hangar before the college took over the whole field. The property owner was ready to chop up all the land and sell it, but he never did. Now, I guess the development company has been giving Dad a heck of a time, trying to take the hangar out from under him."

Barbara rises from her seat and squeezes past me, toward the corner of the office. "I want to show you both something."

Dad and I look at each other as she opens a door right next to a tall bookcase in the corner of the office. I didn't even notice it was there earlier. We both stand up and follow the woman through the door.

I step inside in disbelief. It's an enormous space that I had always assumed was filled with junk. But this side of the metal building is in stark contrast to the messes of newspapers and dirty tools occupying the other side, where I had made a futile attempt to clean.

The floor is painted a cream color and polished to a shine. Three airplanes are parked, facing one another. I recognize one of them. The one with the glass-covered cockpit was at the airfield that I followed Dorothy to. Another is a smaller tail wheel plane with a wooden propeller. The third has a really long nose that sits so high that I wonder how Henry ever got it in here. It nearly touches the high rounded ceiling. How could a pilot maneuver such a thing?

The walls are covered in corkboard and they have laminated newspaper clippings and magazine articles tacked neatly all around. There is a glass case along the entire far wall, filled with things like the headphones Dorothy was wearing when she was flying. There are maps and parachutes and goggles. It's unreal how much stuff is in here.

Dad points to a large plaque covering the rear wall and I walk back to get a closer look. It has pictures of various women, posing in their uniforms next to airplanes or standing outside the very barracks I had walked through. In the center hangs a large black and white photograph of Dorothy and Henry. They are standing next to each other, both wearing wide smiles. Dorothy is leaning into Henry. The caption at the bottom reads, "Once We Were WASPs."

Barbara hands Dad a piece of paper and I watch him read it with tears in his eyes. He looks at me. "I cannot for the life of me explain this." He shakes his head at Barbara. "I don't know what to say."

"What, Dad?"

"Barbara's right, Grace. Henry has willed this hangar with everything in it, as well as the other airplanes he owns on the field, to you and me."

"Seriously?" I look at Barbara.

"Well, Paul, Dad also left behind quite a sum of money to go toward purchasing the rest of the property," Barbara says, standing with her hands on her hips and looking between Dad and me.

"What about you?" I ask her. "Don't you want these things?"

"Ha!" she says. "I told you, my dad was a businessman. He left me plenty. Between his house and that old truck, I have my hands full. I don't want anything to do with this stuff out here."

Barbara winks at me. "Paul," she says, "there is a stipulation in there, in case you aren't interested in taking on all this responsibility."

Dad looks down at the paper, rubbing his chin while reading its contents. "It seems that Henry would like these things to be used to...create a memorial to the WASP organization, a museum of sorts." Dad's eyes shift across the words on the page. "And, it says that if we cannot find a means to do this, then we should follow the proper steps to ensure that these items are donated to an official who represents the WASP organization."

Dad sighs and looks at me. "I didn't even know that the WASP women existed until Barbara handed me this photograph to give to you."

Barbara smiles at me. "You seemed really intrigued by it when you were cleaning his hangar."

Dad slips the picture of Dorothy out from under a sheet of paper and hands it to me.

"Oh," Barbara interrupts, "that reminds me, Grace. Dad had a lot to tell me last night, obviously. But he wanted me to give you this too." She holds out an envelope to me and then gives me a hug. "Thank you. It meant the world that you visited Dad and kept him company in that hospital. He really enjoyed talking to you." Barbara steps back and wipes another tear from her face.

"Well," she says, checking her watch. "I have to go. I have a meeting about Dad's memorial service in ten minutes." Barbara sifts through her keys and Dad moves closer to her, cupping his hand around the top of her arm.

"I'll be in my hangar this afternoon if you need any help, Barbara. And Grace and I would love to give you a hand preparing for your dad's service. Grace's mother would probably like to help out too. She knew your father."

"Thanks, Paul. I'll stop by once I have a better handle on things."

Dad gives Barbara a hug and she smiles shyly before she closes the door, giving us both a quick wave. Then he squats down and runs his hand across the shiny floor. "Wow. What do you think about all this, G? I don't believe it. I'd better call the guys and tell them. We've got some work to do!"

I'm busy trying to figure out how to climb into the airplane with the glass-covered cockpit. It's so cool looking. I wonder how the women even got themselves into it. "Do you think Henry fixed these up by himself, Dad?"

"I have no idea, but I would be amazed if he did. How did I never know what was going on in here, or about the WASP women, or any of this stuff? I mean, you told me about your flight that night and then Barbara said that Henry was a flight instructor for the WASP women during the war. I've been hearing airplanes buzzing around the field in the middle of the night." Dad looks at me. "I don't know what to think, G."

"I know, me too, Dad," I say. I point to the photo of Dorothy and Henry. "That is Dorothy. She's the one I met...the woman I flew with the night that Karl had an accident."

Dad looks at me, calculating my words. "I don't know, G. But I do know that after you told me about Dorothy, I thought of that woman I saw in my hangar. Then a week or so after Karl's accident, I slept on my couch out here and I heard the airplanes again. When Barbara came over and gave me the photo of Dorothy, she told me about the WASP ladies. And that made me want to research when the airport was built and who used to fly here. All I can find is verification that it was opened in the late 1920s, but it seems impossible to track who used it, or what would make it a target for any sort of bizarre...happenings."

I watch him stammer over his words. "Are you talking about ghosts, Dad? Do you think they're ghosts?"

He shrugs. "Grace, when Barbara brought me this picture,

she made me think about your story. And I wondered if there was any possible way that you could be telling the truth."

He walks over to the airplane that I'm standing next to and touches its smooth metal cowling. "You know, Dorothy looks a lot like the woman who wanted to fly that old broken airplane. Now I come in here and that same bird is parked in front of me, in cherry condition. Henry couldn't possibly have done this all by himself!" Dad laughs. "I just don't have an explanation for it, G."

I giggle to myself. This is nuts. But it's the most excited I have ever seen my father.

Dad looks around the room in awe. "Why do you think Henry never opened a museum himself?"

"I'll bet he was just waiting for Dorothy, Dad. I think he collected all of this just to feel closer to her."

Dad looks perplexed. "I'm at a loss for words right now, but maybe these WASP women need to be remembered. Maybe this museum is the right thing to do."

"Yes! I totally agree, Dad. It is a memorial. It's a celebration of what they did, of who they were."

He stares through me, daydreaming.

"Dad," I ask, quietly, "do you sort of believe my story of what happened that night with Dorothy?"

He shakes his head and smiles. "I can't answer that, G. But I think we should keep it a secret for now, what do you say?"

I nod in agreement and instinctively walk outside to get some air, to process all of this.

I forgot about the envelope from Henry. I turn it over and tear it open. There's a note inside.

Dear Grace,

Thank you for listening to my confession. It sure means a lot that you were willing to spend time with an old codger like me. I just have a couple things that I'd like you to know, kid.

Start looking over the manual for the BT-13. Read all my notes and sit in the plane for a long time before you take your first lesson. When you're ready for an instructor, I think you know where to come.

And wait until you get nice and comfortable flying that airplane before you even think about studying the P-51 manual. Have patience, you'll get there. Besides, once you learn that bird, you can fly anything that comes your way.

Don't let anyone steal your fire, kid. You have the power to do whatever you want to in this lifetime. Oh, and don't worry about giving Dorothy the message. I have a feeling she's on her way.

Take care and happy flying,

Henry

The P-51? That must be the massive airplane in the middle of Henry's hangar. Does Henry want me to learn to fly that airplane? Dorothy is on her way, huh?

I look over at Betty and she is standing proud in the corner of the ramp, beneath the cottonwood tree with its few shriveled leaves still clinging to branches. No snow on her wings. The rest of the airplanes out here are blanketed in white. Is that steam coming off her right engine?

About the Author

Judi Stephenson works as a professional pilot based in the beautiful state of Colorado. She grew up at the foot of the Rocky Mountains, where she enjoys hiking and spending time outdoors. Judi began her college studies in music and has performed as a singer/songwriter in various venues, until she discovered her passion for flying. It was while she was working as a flight instructor that the inspiration for this story came to her. And it was when she read about the Women Airforce Service Pilots of World War II that she knew it had to be written. Thank you for reading it.